STAY TOGETHER

PART I

BEFORE THE WAR

BY

JASON DREW ANDERSON

ISBN-13: 979-8-9988601-1-9

Cover design by: Henry Hambardzumyan (Henryyan)

Dedication

First and foremost, I want to thank my daughter, Claire Renee Anderson. She is the reason this book was written. Long ago, when Claire was starting to discover writing and getting into novels, we worked together to create the first piece of this manuscript. In attempting to show her how story writing works, we created this together based on our own family. The characters, Reese and Maverick were her idea, and I based their personalities on the two sides of Claire. First, the shy and anxious side of Reese and the determined and rebellious side of Maverick. Claire is the embodiment of both characters in one. She has been my biggest supporter and motivator in writing this, and it would never have existed without her. This book is dedicated to her in hopes of a bright future ahead.

I would like to thank my wonderful wife, Bonnie Anderson. She had spent many days and nights allowing me to write this story at the cost of neglecting daily chores and responsibilities. She has believed in this story since the start. She has read countless revisions and provided honest feedback that has been crucial to the story creation.

I would like to thank Drew Anderson, Lily Stafford, Finnegan Stafford and Thomas Anderson. They are the other four children in the family and have been an inspiration and very supportive of me writing this story. My mother Louise and brother, Jeremy Anderson for their continued family support.

Tabitha Gagnonn, my main editor, who had inspired and cheered me on to complete the story after it spent over a year on the shelf. Her questions and guidance helped me to get inspired to continue and ultimately complete the story.

Chapter One

13 October

17 days before the war

Archer sat down in the middle of the road and began to cry. This was a big deal and meant things were bad. Archer was the strongest and most stable of the family—even extended family and friends. At seventeen years old, Archer was disciplined and stoic. If he's crying, things must be really bad.

This has been an autumn like no other for the Jenkins family, the entire country, and even the world for that matter. The Pandemic was bad enough. The prices rose and rose, but wages did not. Food was unattainable, except for the most well-off.

The government tried to do something. At least it appeared that way on the news and the internet. Nobody could afford food anymore, and people were hungry. The world was hungry. The Jenkins family was no exception, and if Archer was like this hunger was causing real pain.

Maverick ran out onto the road then abruptly came to a stop when she saw the tears streaming down his face. She was holding it together well, like the rest of the family. But seeing Archer hunched over in the middle of the suburban neighborhood road filled her chest with a sense of dread. She stood petrified as the fear washed over her. She snapped from her trance at the distant flash and delayed boom from an explosion several miles away toward downtown Charlotte.

"Archer! It's getting closer. Let's go inside. Please!" Maverick pleaded. Her teeth were starting to chatter from the chill. Cracks and booms from the distance brought a burning, smoky haze to the air. Archer wiped his eyes and sniffed. He stood up and looked at his little sister who couldn't hold back her tears any longer. Archer put his arm around Maverick, and they silently shuffled back toward the house.

Stan was standing in the doorway watching them in the darkness. He felt like a failure. His children didn't feel safe. They weren't safe. That used to be the cardinal sin of the modern parent. 'Don't let your kids feel unsafe.' Rules of the past now. Stan couldn't help it, though. He couldn't accept this was happening any more than anyone else could.

"Come on, guys. Let's go," he hushed out as loud as he dared. Maverick and Archer came back through the door. Stan quickly closed and locked it behind them.

He was still clenching the letter in his hand. He leaned his back against the door and re-read it.

ORDER TO REPORT FOR INDUCTION... Jenkins, Archer... You are hereby ordered for induction into the Armed Forces of the United States, and to report at...

Stan couldn't believe this draft notice even got delivered to the home, or that there was still a working Postal Service. Why didn't he get a draft notice? Is 49 too old?

Chapter Two

27 August

429 days before the war

"I'm not going to say it again, you guys. Get down here!" Lexi shouted up the stairs. Loud thumps and unintelligible shouts echoed off the upstairs walls and ceiling. "Come on, Stan! Get your butt up."

Stan lifted his head with a face of feigned agony and seemed to slide further into the couch. After he caught Lexi's stern and impatient glare, he puffed out an obvious sigh and clicked the TV off. Slowly and dramatically, he rose to his feet. The world was just so unfair. Stan was lazy on the weekends. That's what he called it. He needed to be. During the weekdays, he would work his full-time job followed by side work on top of that some nights.

"Yep yep!" he chirped with a forced smile, trying to get himself motivated. Stan looked at his phone and checked the credit card balances. He had done this three or four times over the last hour but checked again.

Lexi flashed a look and said, "This is important."

Stan nodded and whispered, "I know, but so is food." He gave a quick wink and a smile.

Maverick and Reese raced down the stairs side by side, bumping each other into the wall and handrail on the way down. The low and methodical thump of Archer's big feet strolling down the stairs followed last. He appeared to have just woken from a nap. He held up his phone, typing away with his thumbs and traversed slowly down the steps.

"Alright, guys. We're gonna make this as quick and speedy as possible. We need two shirts and two pairs of pants," Lexi instructed sternly.

Reese disappointedly dropped her shoulders, "That's it?"

"That's it. Nothing more, nothing less. You guys still have plenty of clothes," Lexi declared, attempting to quell any more objections. The kids groaned in agreement except for Archer who stayed glued to his phone. Lexi snatched the phone from Archer's hand, "You can take a break from your girlfriend for a couple of hours." Reese, Maverick, and Archer were getting ready for 6th, 7th, and 11th grade, respectively.

"Come on! Let's Go!" Lexi screamed up the stairs. Leo and Blaze crashed down on the landing, fighting with each other. Leo, the youngest, still had another year before kindergarten. He was born just a few days after the school-age cutoff. His older brother Blaze was ready for 1st grade this year. Blaze may have been the older of the two, but they looked the same age and size.

The Jenkins family had a structured routine for loading up the minivan. Leo first—strapped in by Archer—then Blaze, followed by Reese, Maverick, then Archer. Lexi always drove. Stan didn't have the temperament for Charlotte traffic, so he only drove when he had to.

"How's the gas?" Stan asked, peering over to peek at the needle on the dashboard. Lexi threw the minivan in reverse and sped down the driveway. "Well, we have enough to get there and back. That's a 'tomorrow' problem."

Gas was the highest the state had ever seen—the country, for that matter. Traffic was bad. It wasn't just back-to-school time traffic.

Traffic was getting worse overall in the crowded metro area. Charlotte, located in Mecklenburg County, had exploded in population since 2010. The roads and infrastructure were slow to keep up.

"I need shoes!" Maverick shouted from the back.

"Your shoes are fine." Stan retorted.

"We can try to take a look," Lexi yelled back.

Stan rolled his eyes knowing she was trying to placate the children and keep the kids optimistic.

They reached the outdoor mall and were able to find a spot to park at—what seemed— nearly a quarter mile away. The mall was crowded and bustling with parents and kids with the same plan.

Lexi put the minivan in park and turned around to face the kids. "It's really crowded. What's the rule?"

"STAY TOGETHER," the kids groaned in unison.

The mall was on the outskirts of Charlotte, between the downtown area and their home in the suburbs. It was self-proclaimed to be an outlet mall for big brand names at a supposed discount. It became a widely known place where one was more likely to find goods in stock. Shipments of goods were sporadic, and you often just had to rely on social media updates from the stores.

You'd have thought it was a popular amusement park on the 4th of July. It was hot, humid and hard to move. Maverick grabbed Reese's hand for support when she noticed her becoming anxious.

"I want a corndog!" Leo yelled.

"No! I want a corndog!" Blaze competed.

Stan held up a finger to both of them, "Silence, children!"

Lexi rolled her eyes at her husband, "Yes, very effective, Stan."

"Why is it so crazy here?" Archer asked, scanning around at the stores and crowds waiting outside.

Lexi stated quickly, "I don't know. I just really want to check on Old Navy. That's what I saw online. They supposedly just got a large shipment this morning. Let's just get in and get out, okay?"

The smaller stores had set up lines to limit the number of customers inside. The larger stores with higher customer capacity typically wouldn't set up lines outside since it was nearly impossible to keep track of capacity. This often resulted in very crowded spaces when shopping inside them. Prices were high, availability of goods was scarce, and the ever-worsening labor shortages made for long waits and plenty of disappointed customers. At least half the shops were empty or closed until further notice.

News feeds over the past month were droning endlessly about the problems facing the country. It was difficult to understand what the real problem was. The media seemed to push their own stories and called their opinions facts. The only certainty was that prices were out of control and products were becoming less and less available.

"Here, let's go!" Stan held the door open for the family to finally file into a packed clothing store. People were shoulder to shoulder and grumbling loudly. The shelves were sparse. Clothing was scattered and picked through. Lexi took Maverick and Reese by the hands and marched them toward the women's clothing. It was too crowded. Lexi tried to peer at what was on the shelves.

Suddenly, three women arguing over a pair of jeans broke into a pushing match. The arguing quickly escalated to screaming. The pushing escalated to slapping. Then one of the women had lost her hold of the pants and tackled the other woman, knocking into Maverick who fell onto the floor with them. Reese screamed. The third woman tried to take advantage of the fight and grabbed the jeans. Several onlookers were screaming at them to stop and began grabbing and pushing the women.

Lexi pushed herself into the melee and pulled Maverick up to her feet. She put her arm around Maverick and pulled her away from the fight. Reese stood frozen. Lexi grabbed Reese by the hand and pulled her away as well. Stan was holding Blaze and Leo's hands. They were starting to cry.

Lexi brought the girls over toward them. "This is too much, we just have to make do with what we have."

The minivan was quiet on the way home. Maverick sat with her arm around Reese to calm her down. They both said they were okay but were clearly still afraid. None of the kids in the Jenkins family had ever really seen any kind of real-life violence, just stuff in movies and on social media. Neither Maverick nor Reese was using their phones in the van, which was very rare.

Reese, whose real name was Renee, spent many months and great effort getting everyone to call her Reese. This happened rather suddenly last school year, when she was struggling with getting bullied by her peers, mostly because of the severe acne on her face. Her big sister Mavis insisted on changing her name to Maverick in solidarity. Maverick always chafed at the old-fashionedness of her given name anyway and seized the moment to use a name she liked better. While it was usually Reese who copied her big sister's every move, she did appreciate the unconditional support of her big sister. Over the summer, the family and everyone else in their lives got used to the new names, although Maverick's name naturally got shortened from Maverick to Mav.

When the family returned home, everyone ran back to their rooms. Lexi told them to get out the clothes they currently had so she could take an inventory and maybe try again another day. Delivery services online were backed up for weeks to months. The Jenkinses themselves had several orders for various purchases that just never arrived. It was quiet for the rest of the day and into the evening. This was the first sting of reality the family had faced with the changing world.

"Alright, they're in bed," Stan said, dropping himself on the sofa next to Lexi. It had been his turn to put Leo and Blaze to bed this week. She was scrolling through her phone as Archer lay across the loveseat watching TV. The girls were in their rooms upstairs, as usual.

Stan looked over at his wife. "So?"

"Hmm?" she let out with her eyes still glued to her phone.

"That was quite an experience at the mall—"

"Still don't want to talk about it."

Stan shrugged his shoulders and looked at the TV.

"There's been riots in Charlotte. You know, it could have been worse," Archer chimed in, scrolling his phone as well.

"Can you turn the TV off if you're watching your phone, you can't do both." Stan snapped.

"I'm just saying, there's videos all over. Evelyn sent me a few. She said there was—"

"Well, there's videos of anything you want to find." Stan replied.

"Well, what about groceries?" Archer asked, setting his phone down.

"We're okay, don't worry—"

"Can't we just talk about this?" Archer protested.

Lexi put her phone down and looked up at them both. She let out a sigh. "Okay. Fine. Let's talk about it."

It went quiet as they all looked at each other. Finally, Stan clapped his hands, "Okay! Okay, let's talk about it." He stood up and went to the kitchen table. With a flourish, he swung his arm for Lexi and Archer to follow him. They reluctantly moved to the table. Stan scrolled through his phone and displayed it at the table for them to see. "Allow me to present our budget," Stan grinned, waiting for a response. He cleared his throat and continued. "These are what the grocery costs were last year. This is this year. This is two weeks ago."

Archer leaned and squinted at the screen. "That's a lot, right?"

Stan withdrew his phone and changed to another screen, "Well, this is how much I make. This is how much we owe for expenses and such. So, this is what's left over. It's quite a math problem. For sure."

Lexi didn't look at the screen.

Archer sat and rubbed his chin, "so we need to make more money?"

Stan gave a thoughtful look. He liked to see the kids use their brains. He saw this as an opportunity. "That would be nice. I'm already working a fulltime job and part time sessions at night, contracting. Your mother had to quit her job. Daycare costed more than she made in salary and gas. On top of all that, we've pretty much maxed out the credit cards and we're burning through retirement money to stay afloat."

Archer nodded. "I could find a job."

Lexi and Stan looked at each other and nodded, "That could help. It could help some, but you see the costs here. Food is astronomical. I think if you could pay for your own gas and dates with your girlfriend, that would actually help a lot."

Lexi grunted, "They've got to do something, it can't stay like this. Nobody can buy food or anything!"

"There's not much food to be sold anymore. At least right now." Stan calmly replied.

"We should grow our own food then," Archer added.

"Do you know how to do that? Grow it where?" Stan challenged.

"We can figure it out. Like you said, you can find videos on anything."

Stan hated when people used his own words against him, but from Archer, he found it to be clever. "We can try, I suppose. Neither of us know anything about that. It would be a lot of work, and we're pretty busy most of the time."

Archer sat for a moment thinking, then stood up determined, "I got this," he said and headed upstairs with his phone and laptop.

Lexi and Stan shared a look and reached for each other's hand.

"What do you think is going to happen?" Lexi asked.

Stan smiled and shrugged his shoulders. "I think it's all going to be okay."

Lexi stood up and pulled her laptop off the counter where it had been charging and brought it back to the table. Stan sighed dramatically as he watched her change gears. He knew his wife well. As soon as the kids were in bed and out of sight and earshot, she would become obsessed when she was worried. "Sweetheart, don't. It's not going to help."

Lexi was ignoring him and started scanning through her news feed. This wasn't the first time she'd done this since prices started to rise. Stan's pleading continued. "You know there are no answers. It's the modern-day internet. More noise and words than ever and no way to know what's real or not. Even from the 'trusted' news sources."

She continued staring at the screen like he wasn't there. The last time she did this was when the proxy wars across the globe started. The United States was committed financially and sent military forces overseas to support NATO. Europe and Asia were entrenched in war, and the U.S. was funding it through money, arms, and troops. As a result, the cost of imports skyrocketed as well as the federal deficit. There was a time in Stan's life where the subjects of politics and government fiscal management were very interesting. That interest disappeared when Archer was born. Now his focus was his family and keeping them away from this

14

kind of worry and anxiety, so he often avoided talking about or even listening to the news.

"It's like there's three narratives going on here," Lexi whispered to herself, as Stan was still not being helpful in her opinion. "The mainstream media just says everything is fine and it's all in our heads, or it's all one party's fault or the other, and the worst—is that revolution is coming."

"See! That's what I'm saying," Stan found his footing. This kind of thing has happened in the past, and there's nothing we can do about it." She continued to ignore him. "I love you. I'm going to bed. Please sleep," Stan said in defeat as he got up from the table and headed to bed.

Chapter Three

14 October

16 days before the war

It was just past midnight. Stan was still standing against the front door. It was dark and quiet in the house. He checked the lock again and peeked out of the blinds into the darkness. He walked into the open dining area and sat at the table. Lexi was sitting there alone, staring into the flame of an oil lamp. All the kids were asleep in the living room. Stan withdrew the revolver from the holster laying on the table, checked the cylinder with a spin and put it back in the holster where it had been. The revolver had stayed out of the safe for several weeks now. Checking it was Stan's new habit. It helped him think.

"Where's Archer?" Stan asked.

"Upstairs."

"What are we going to do?"

Lexi didn't answer. She continued to stare.

"I'm sorry," Stan lamented.

Tears rolled down her face as she continued to stare. Stan put his hands to his forehead. "I can figure this out," he whispered. Standing up, he lit a lantern and headed upstairs. Stan quietly knocked on Archer's door and slowly opened it. He could see Archer sitting on his bed illuminated by a flickering candle.

"Hey," Archer said quietly.

Stan entered the room and softly closed the door behind him. He set the lantern down next to the candle and exposed the wick to brighten the light. "Come on!" Stan whispered. "We have to hurry." Stan went into Archer's closet and grabbed an empty duffel bag. He set it on the bed and started to open the dresser drawers.

"I'm taking you to Grandad's. It's far enough away. You'll be able to—"

"Dad!"

"There's barely even a government or army. They won't even look for—"

"Dad!"

Stan stopped and looked at Archer. "You're not going."

"I have to."

"No."

"Dad, I have to go."

"Why? Is this just because of Evelyn?"

"Come on, we've been over that. It's not just about her. You know what's happening. War is coming. I know you want to keep us all out of it. We can't stay together forever—"

"Yes, we can—"

"No, Dad. We can't. I have to do this. I'll be okay, I promise."

Stan sat down next to Archer on the bed and started to cry. Archer put his arm around his dad. Seeing his father cry was painful, and he couldn't hold back his own tears.

Chapter Four

3 September

422 days before the war

Today was the first day of school. Stan had already left the house to drop Blaze off on his way to the clinic. Archer was driving now and would be taking Reese and Maverick as well. The middle school was on the way to the high school, just a few hundred yards down the road. This made sense, Lexi would tell herself. She was still worried. She gave Archer at least two short lectures in the last 24 hours about driving safely, not diverting from the route she had established, and not stopping to pick up friends or Evelyn. Archer was good at looking receptive when she talked about it.

Reese and Mav sat in the backseat. His mother insisted they sit in the back and would drone on and on about statistics of injury in the front seat versus the back seat—Archer thought it was silly. It worked out better for him though, since he wouldn't need to hear their endless chatter as much. Mav and Reese found the ride adventurous. They'd been in the car when Archer drove before but not without adults.

"Listen, you guys," Archer shouted toward the back seat. Reese and Mav were briefly reminded of their dad. Archer turned the music down, and lowered the volume of his voice. "After school, just wait by the statue. Don't go to the pickup line. I'll be a little late getting there today."

The girls both looked at each other. "What about the route? What Mom said?" Reese asked.

"I'm not changing the route home. She didn't say anything about *before* I pick you guys up, just after."

"Why?" Mav asked.

"Don't worry about it." Archer knew that wouldn't be enough. "I have to see someone right after school about a job."

"You're getting a job?" they both exclaimed in unison.

"Where?"

"Does Mom know?"

"Are you quitting school?"

Archer groaned as the questions persisted without pause for answers. He finally interrupted them. "Yes! Mom knows. It's going to be in the evenings and weekends. Look, I'm just going to be about fifteen minutes late. I'll let Mom know."

Mav was suspicious. She was always suspicious. "So, you're telling Mom after or before?"

"Mavis!"

"It's Maverick!" Both girls shouted back in unison.

Archer ignored their protest, "I'll tell Mom after. *And,* I'm asking you guys to do the same, okay? Forgiveness over permission." Now he definitely sounded like his dad. Stan's favorite mantra, forgiveness over permission meant it's better to do something and later apologize for it than to ask for permission and be told 'no.' Of course, his dad was always referring to his work and didn't really mean for his children to use it on them.

Mav and Reese were dropped off at the middle school. This was Reese's first year at the new school, and she was extremely nervous. Mav already knew the ins and outs of the school. This was Reese's first time setting foot.

Reese always had a lot of trouble interacting with other kids because she was so shy and often had her sister talk for her. Last year, the teasing began just as she started to develop persistent acne on her face. Reese's classmates took advantage of it when Maverick moved to the middle school and made fun of her relentlessly, as Mav wasn't there to protect her. She was very relieved to be back with Mav this year, even if it was an entirely new school. She stayed close to Mav, who led the way in.

It was mostly Mav doing all the talking—as usual—as they walked into the busy hallway, reuniting with friends from last year. They split apart just before the bell rang for homeroom.

Mav sat near the back of the class where she could find an empty seat. She started to feel tense as she scanned the room and realized there were no friends in here. It started to feel like everyone was watching her. Mav sat at her desk and searched for something in her backpack to fidget with—she got bored easily. The whiteboard in front of the class had six words, 'NO PHONES. I WILL TAKE THEM.' Mav couldn't help but notice everyone seemed to obey. Probably because it was the first day of school.

Mav felt a pencil tap on her shoulder. She turned around to see a girl with a backward baseball cap on her head. "Hello, my name is Willow. I am pleased to meet you," she said in a sarcastic almost robotic voice with a forced cheesy smile. She dropped the smile, "There! Now I can tell my mother I socialized today." Mav chuckled.

"It's nice to meet you. I'm Maverick."

"Ha! That's a good one."

"No, I'm serious. Are you new here?"

"Yeah, just moved to the area. Wait, I'm sorry, Maverick? Like from the movie?"

"No, like an independent thinker."

"Uh-huh," Willow was trying to hold back laughter. "Well, it's nice to meet you... Maverick."

Mav smiled and turned back toward the front of the room. At lunch, Reese was awkwardly searching for Mav at the tables. She felt a huge relief when she spotted her sister. She scurried over to the empty seat next to her. "I don't have anyone from last year in any of my classes." Reese unloaded. "I can't find where anything is in this place. I've been late to every class." She pulled and twirled a lock of her long brown hair. She did this when she was feeling anxious.

Mav could see it and just smiled. "Well, it's not great for me either, all my friends are on the first lunch period and I don't have any of them in my classes. It's like I'm new here too." A few minutes later, Maverick spotted Willow who was looking around, unsure where to go. Mav waved her over.

"Oh, well hello again, Maverick." Willow said, still with a little sarcasm.

"Hi! Have a seat. This is my sister—"

Your sister? Let me guess, Goose?"

"No, I'm Reese."

"Ahhhaa!" Willow replied, watching the joke float over Reese's head.

"So where did you move from, anyway?" Mav asked.

"Oh, not far. We moved from Charlotte. We actually moved last spring, but I finished the year at my old school. My parents wanted to get out of the city."

"Why?" Reese asked.

"Because my parents think the world is going to end and we have a better chance out here. Duh!" Willow answered sarcastically.

"What do you mean?" Reese asked with a confused look.

"Well, you know. All the crazy stuff in the world. They think a war is coming. A revolution. They think the food shortages are going to get worse and worse, you know?"

Mav and Reese didn't really know. Willow withdrew a sandwich from her bag. "Don't you guys watch the news or anything?"

The girls shook their heads.

Willow took a bite from her sandwich, "We moved to a bigger house with more land to like, grow food, and raise chickens and all that. It's actually my grandparents' home. Also, it was getting too expensive to live on our own. So, yeah. Here I am."

Reese was mainly focused on her talking with her mouth full. She started to twirl her hair again.

Reese looked at Mav, "Do you think that could actually happen?"

"I think people like my parents panic a lot," Willow answered before Maverick could.

"Well, I sure hope so." Mav answered, "Everything will be okay," she said, attempting to reassure her sister. She didn't want another worry added to the pile.

***

22

Archer had been able to clear the last period of his day, allowing him to leave early. His school day also ended 30 minutes before the middle school to stagger traffic in the area. He was glad to get back to school but was focused on finding a job. The conversation the other night about the family's financial problems was just one of the reasons.

He had been trying to find a good time to ask. That conversation made the perfect opportunity. He didn't say anything more to his parents than he needed to but had talked to his friend Miles who worked at a local hardware store. They desperately needed help there. He was able to apply and set up an interview for that afternoon. A good word from his friend working there didn't hurt either.

As he walked in through the front of the school entry, he saw Evelyn leaning against a pillar. Her long brunette hair blowing in the breeze made him feel warm inside and almost electric when he saw her smile at him.

"Hey, there," he said in a cheesy voice. Evelyn giggled and ran up to him, wrapping her arms around him.

"Well, the one good thing about school is I get to see you every day," she said before giving him a kiss.

Evelyn was a senior this year. They'd met the year before. Oddly, it wasn't at school. They met at a movie theatre where she had worked last summer. Archer had an instant crush when he met her and was going to see movies nearly every day for a week just to talk to her in the confection line. He'd gotten the courage to ask her on a date, which she agreed to. They'd been together since.

Walking down the crowded hallway, Archer put his arm around Evelyn. She continued to smile. "Who do you have for U.S. History? That's my first class, I couldn't take it last year," Evelyn said, looking at her schedule on her phone.

"Augar, I think. He nearly failed me in World History. Hopefully, he doesn't remember me."

"Of course he does! Who wouldn't?" Evelyn stopped in front of him and put her arms around his neck. "This is my first class right here. Be good!" She kissed him on the lips and walked off. Archer stood watching her walk into class. She made him feel alive.

"There's my man!" A boisterous voice came from behind.

"Miles. Welcome back!" Archer grinned and threw his arm around Miles's shoulder and playfully pulled him into a headlock.

"Got your interview today? Remember to mention me."

"Right after school, I'm gonna leave a bit early."

"Oh, I passed Mr. Augar in the hall, he was asking where you were."

"What?"

Miles burst into laughter, "I'm just messing with you."

***

Although Archer didn't have a class at the end of the day, he wasn't supposed to leave early. The student parking lot gate was locked during school hours. He had parked down the road and snuck out of the school after his last class, dodging the resource officer who roamed the halls.

"What's your availability?" Don asked with a gruff voice. His white beard was tarnished yellow from years of nicotine. He lit up a cigarette outside in the parking lot where he met Archer.

"I can work from 4:30 until you close during the week and anytime on the weekend."

"Are you sure? Everyone says that. Then sure enough, it becomes only Tuesday and needing every weekend off—"

"No sir, that's my availability. It won't change."

"Mm-hmm. You don't have any experience."

"No, I don't—not a formal job, but I've been a hard worker my whole life, I'm always on time, I follow—"

"Minimum wage."

"That's just fine, sir. I know when you see my work—"

"Start Friday, be here at 4:30 to fill out paperwork and get your vest and schedule." Don barked, flicking his cigarette onto the parking lot. "Welcome aboard!" He exclaimed walking back into the store. Archer discreetly pumped his fist and ran back to his car with a big smile on his face. He rushed to get his sisters at the middle school before they started to panic.

***

Stan was a clinical social worker. He had graduated with a master's degree in social work in his twenties and mostly worked for county social services agencies following graduation. He loved the work but it was tough and underappreciated. The pay was low and advancement was limited. He grew frustrated with the internal politics and competition over the severely limited supervisor positions. As their family grew, so did the family's need for additional income.

With Lexi's support and encouragement, Stan had become a licensed clinical social worker and therapist. It wasn't easy, involving three years and a temporary step back in pay. It felt like ten years to him, but he was glad he did it—even if his mom still told people he was a psychiatrist.

Stan was the clinical director for a moderately sized community mental health agency called Behavioral Health For All—most commonly known as BHFA. Clinical director sounded important, but what it really meant was he filled in all the gaps when people quit. Turnover was extremely high, the pay wasn't worth it and the work was very thankless. Most of Stan's day was providing assessments and therapy for walk-in clients. Most of his agency's clients were poor, uninsured, and very ill. Stan never turned anyone away, insured or not. That would sometimes come back to bite him from the administrators. Over the past several months, as prices really got high, Stan contracted with two other agencies in the evenings doing virtual therapy. It was tiring.

After wrapping up his final session of the day, he started to pack his bag to go home.

"Stan?" came a familiar voice from across the office. Stan stuck his head out the door. Ruth, the clinic's receptionist, was standing over her desk. "Hey, um… there's someone here to see you."

Stan couldn't see the window from where he was standing. He let out a sigh, "Alright. Hold on."

"As I live and breathe!" Stan let out when he caught sight of the visitor. Brenda Long, stood in the empty waiting room.

She simply gave a smile and waved, "Hey, Stan." Brenda was a long-time coworker at Gaston County Social Services. Stan hadn't seen her in at least 4 years. He waved her back to his office and she followed. Stan lifted several stacks of files and binders off a chair for her to sit down.

"Ha, it's been a long time. Still with the County I see," he peered at the badge pinned to her suit.

Brenda laughed, "Yeah, I'm still there. Moved out of social services though, I'm running the Office of Emergency Management now."

"Oh, I see. Well, you're wearing your nametag, so I'm guessing this isn't a social visit."

"No, no, it's not. I'm here to see if you can help out with something." Brenda's smile and tone became a little more serious.

"I don't really want to go back to the county, the private sector is really treating me well, as you can plainly see." Stan joked.

Brenda let out a forced chuckle and smile. "No, it's not like that. Emergency Management is in charge of staffing committees, and I was wondering if you could, well, staff a committee."

Stan groaned. "You know I hate committees."

"I do. I remember. This is a little different. It's an important one." Brenda said with a straight face.

"There's no such thing as an important committee."

Brenda continued to stare, ignoring his jab.

"Okay, I'm listening," he said, realizing he was being too much.

"We have some big changes that are going to be happening. It has to do with SNAP and WIC—and everyone really."

"What do you mean?"

"Well, it's a planning committee. We need to plan for county food distribution. Just in case it's needed."

"What? Like rationing?"

"We prefer to call it distribution."

"You said 'in case it's needed.' Is it needed?"

"I don't know. I can tell you the forces from above have made this my number one priority, so—I don't know. They don't tell me everything." Brenda paused and opened her planner. "I'm forming committees and subcommittees for the LEPC," she continued.

"The what?"

"Local Emergency Planning Committee."

"Why me? I don't work for the county."

"We need people in the community. The stakeholders, providers. You're the clinical director here. We've worked together and you're pretty levelheaded. If something like this gets rolled out, we need cooperation and input from businesses, service providers, public sector, private sector."

"I appreciate that, Brenda, but I really have a lot on my plate with the family and working three jobs and all."

"I hear you. Just think about it. Read this over. It will give the details about what we need and how you'd be compensated. This might be a big deal, Stan. Oh, and no rush, but I need an answer by next Monday."

Stan glanced over the folder Brenda handed him. He turned a couple of pages as Brenda stood up to leave. "Brenda, can you tell me a little more about what's going on? I'd like to hear it from you."

Brenda smiled. It appeared she was choosing her words carefully. "Well, to put it simply, there may come a time when there's not enough food and supplies to meet demand. We need to make sure that everyone has an opportunity to buy the goods they need. We're putting a plan in place to make sure there's equal distribution for everyone."

***

Lexi was rushing to finish dinner. She'd spent the day taking care of Leo and picking up Blaze from his first day of school. She was exhausted, but it was a relief to have all the kids back at school and only have to entertain one during the day.

Lexi had become a master of making a lot with a little. What usually required an entire packet of chicken was now completed by chopping up one or two chicken breasts and adding lots of canned vegetables. Especially corn—lots of corn.

The family sat for dinner at the kitchen table. This was a nightly ritual, not because of wholesome family values, but because the little boys had ruined two couches and the carpet with their spills.
The kids groaned at the sight of more corn, and they were quickly shushed by Lexi. Stan came running down the stairs after finishing a virtual therapy session with a client. He made a dramatic entrance into the kitchen and to his seat. He clapped his hands, "Woohoo, let's eat! Alright! First day of school for everyone. Let's hear it!"

"Archer got a job!" Reese shouted.

Archer rolled his eyes to the ceiling, "Renee!"

"It's Reese," the girls retorted in unison.

"What are they talking about?" Lexi asked.

"I was going to tell you, if she hadn't opened her mouth and just minded her own business. Besides, we talked about this the other night."

"I believe I said it wasn't a terrible idea. I thought we'd talk a little more." Stan said sternly.

"How and where did you get a job?" Lexi asked.

"Miles helped me. I'm going to be working on the weekends at Screws and Planks."

"Screws and Planks? The dumpy hardware store?"

"Yeah, just stocking shelves, and I'm hoping to work in the nursery there," Archer answered.

"Why?"

"So, I can learn how to garden and get access to supplies."

Lexi rolled her eyes. Archer set down his fork and was getting visibly upset. "We talked about this. You said none of us know how to grow a garden, and that's why we aren't doing it, and we need food."

Stan turned toward Archer in his seat, "Actually, that is not what I said and not the reason why."

"We need to grow our own food?" Blaze asked innocently.

Lexi shook her head at Blaze, "Just keep eating, Sweetheart. We'll talk about this later. Okay. Now everyone just eat."

It was silent.

"I met a new friend today at school. Her name's Willow. She just moved here from Charlotte." Mav nervously interjected.

Lexi looked up at her and smiled, "That's great! Tell me about her."

Before Mav could answer, Reese blurted out, "They moved here because they need to grow their own food and were going to starve to death in Charlotte."

Lexi groaned, "Oh, come on!"

"See!" Archer yelled. Everyone started talking and yelling at once.

Stan started clapping his hands excitedly, "That's enough! That's enough!"

The rest of dinner was silent. As everyone cleared their plates and made their way upstairs, Lexi and Stan were putting leftovers away and loading the dishwasher. Lexi was obviously frustrated. Stan didn't say anything. He wasn't sure what to say. He stepped in front of her and rubbed her shoulders. She closed her eyes, trying to enjoy it, then gave him a hug.

"We don't need everyone freaking out and getting scared," she finally said. "We need to talk to Archer and put a stop to this, he's going a little overboard. Can we talk to him?"

Stan nodded in agreement. "Hey, one second. Before we say anything. I want to tell you about what happened at work today."

Chapter Five

15 October

15 days before the war

This morning felt safe. At least compared to yesterday and the day before. Lexi stood on the porch watching the sun come up. She didn't see any smoke. The last few days, Charlotte, as well as the small local town of Gastonia, had seen several riots over food and the draft. Here, miles away in their neighborhood, it was calm. She knew everyone was home right now. It felt safe.

In a handful of days, Archer would be gone. She felt it to her core like it had already happened. She didn't know how or why, but it felt like he was already gone. She wanted to keep him home or even move the family far away. She felt like she had no control over anything anymore.

She could see one of The Neighbors *approaching the porch. She walked up the driveway with a rifle slung over her shoulder.*

"Hey, Lexi, good morning," Phoebe said, walking up the driveway with a wave.

Lexi set her mug down on the porch railing and picked up the Mossberg shotgun. "Good morning," she answered. "Ready to go?"

Phoebe stopped before the walkway of the porch and dramatically stretched her arms and arched her back, "Not really, but yeah, let's do it."

The Neighbors, *they called themselves, were the roving neighborhood watch that formed about 9 months ago after home break-ins started to become a daily occurrence. Phoebe lived at the end of the street with her husband Frank and her four-year-old son. She had a handheld HAM radio clipped to her belt that chirped occasionally.*

"How you holding up?" Phoebe asked, breaking the silence. News about the recent delivery of draft notices had spread quickly. Many others had received induction notices the day before as well.

"How'd it go last night?" Lexi asked, ignoring Phoebe's question.

"Frank said everything was fine on his shift last night. I had this on all night and just heard the other shifts check in, so it looks like everything's okay. Not over there, though." Phoebe pointed toward the city where some light pillars of smoke could be seen. Lexi didn't respond. Phoebe was feeling uneasy, and it made her chatty. "We're supposed to have power today at one o'clock."

Lexi chuckled, "Yeah, I got that email too. We'll see. They haven't been keeping up with the schedule."

Phoebe and Lexi followed a determined route they had memorized on their roving patrol. There were several different routes, all different paths. Every fifteen minutes, they'd receive a codeword on the radio when they checked in that told them the route to take. They'd change the codewords every few days. There were over 60 adults and older teens who worked together with The Neighbors. *Over the months, it had become well-coordinated and scheduled.*

The Forest View Housing Development was rather secluded, with only two main roads going in and out. There were over 300 homes on the eleven blocks. The development was built in the early 2000's which was meant to be part of a massive development of over 1500 homes spread out through the base of the foothills. When the housing crisis hit in 2008, the development was abandoned, so all that remained were the 300 or so homes along the South Fork River between the Charlotte Metro area and the mountains.

Phoebe and Lexi reached the end of the route and paused for a moment to radio in to get the next route, which was given in alphanumeric code and previously memorized. As they started to turn a corner, just before the east end of Forest View Elementary School, Lexi touched Phoebe on the arm, "Wait, look at this."

Phoebe let out a moan, "Not again! That's going to bring us some unwanted attention."

Lexi led Phoebe into the parking lot of the empty elementary school building. Along a broad wall of the gym that faced toward the river was a spray-painted symbol of an upside-down, three-point crown in orange paint, with the message 'BY FORCE IF NECESSARY.' Phoebe used the radio to alert what they found.

Chapter Six

16 September

409 days before the war

Stan pulled Maverick's foot to drag her out of bed. Her alarm had been going off for fifteen minutes already and Reese was already dressed and downstairs along with Archer. "Come on, Mav! You're gonna be late," Stan yelled as she grunted and clung to the mattress.

Stan ran downstairs buttoning his shirt. Lexi was helping Blaze get his shoes on while Archer and Reese were eating cereal. She consoled Blaze who was worried and crying about an impending earthquake he was convinced was going to happen at school. Lexi cursed Stan under her breath for letting him watch that disaster movie with the big kids several weeks ago. Blaze was now scared to death of earthquakes.

"Hey, Dad!" Archer shouted from the kitchen table. "Can you watch this video? It's about quick ways to change your lawn into a garden."

"Not now, Archer. I need to get going. Just text it to me."

"Did you see the other ones I sent you?" Archer asked.

Stan sighed. "Not yet. I'm going to. I will."

Morning routines were challenging even during the summer, but during the school year, it was downright chaotic. Stan and Blaze would leave the house by 7:30 a.m. then Archer and the girls had to be on the road no later than 7:45 a.m.

Mondays at 8:30 a.m. That was the time Lexi learned she had to be at the supermarket if she were to have a chance of getting any kind of meat or produce. She tried to get there even earlier, to be waiting and ready. She was cutting it close, pulling into the parking lot of Food Towne USA at about 8:20 a.m. The parking lot was already full. She wrestled Leo out of the back, and they jogged to the front door. There was only one grocery cart remaining. A long line had already formed at the back of the store.

Leo was whining—she tried to keep him as calm and quiet as she could. They'd had three conversations already about why he couldn't walk on his own in the store due to past behaviors that resulted in tantrums.

As she moved through the line and finally got to the meat section, she saw the sign that limited 2 lbs. for each purchase. She was able to find chicken quarters, and that was all. The rest of the store was extremely bare. Red signs with purchase limits were posted over every product. She was making about four trips per week to three different stores, trying to time restocking as best she could. Eggs and dairy had been unavailable all summer. Their most available products were canned vegetables, frozen fruits and vegetables and name-brand organic products. The prices were extremely high. During this trip, she was able to get almond butter, but it cost $26 for the jar. Many of the processed, shelf foods were available as well, but they often required ingredients that they were running low on.

"Hey there!" Came a woman's voice from behind while in the freezer section.

Lexi turned around and saw her neighbor Phoebe. "Oh, hey Phoebe!" Lexi forced a smile.

"What's it like not being a teacher this year? Enjoying the stay-at-home life?"

"Oh, yes. Nothing better. I get to stay home with this one while Stan gets to live his best life."

"Awe, it can't be all that bad?"

Lexi then remembered that Phoebe was a stay-at-home mom as well. She regretted her last statement. "Oh yeah! I'm totally just joking around." She attempted to recover. "I'm struggling with grocery shopping, though. Just can't find anything, and the cost is just crushing us."

"I know it. I make six trips every week. Just trying to find stuff in stock." Phoebe explained. "So, do you miss teaching yet?"

Lexi nodded, "Yeah, I do. Things have got to go back to normal. I want to work again. I honestly don't know if this is what I'm good at." They chatted for a few minutes more before parting ways.

Phoebe continued down the aisles as Lexi waited in line to pay. Nearly every customer ended up in an argument about the limits on purchases and grumbled about the so-called 'low-low Food Towne USA prices.' Lexi had made many changes to their usual repertoire and menu with cheaper ingredients. She used to buy olive oil, but now corn or vegetable oil was all she could find. She was able to get about half the cart filled up, which was better than most days. The total came to over $450. She had to use two credit cards to complete the transaction.

On the way back from the store, she received a text from Stan. He had been sending her messages about the local food pantries since he worked closely with them. When they scheduled re-supply days—which were often random—he'd text Lexi to see if she could try to get in line. She saw the text, and it gave the address for one that she'd been to in the past. She decided to try. By the time she got there, the line wrapped around the street. She knew they'd be out of stock by the time she got to the front.

***

During the fifteen-minute break after 3rd period, Mav would usually meet Reese and Willow between the main corridor and the gym on the outside grass. It was the central hub between all their separate classes. Reese was always there first. "Reese, how do you get here so fast?" Mav asked, walking across the grass toward her.

"I don't know, I walk fast, I guess. I hate being in the hallways, it's way too crowded."

"There's Mav and Reese!" Willow shouted.

"Hi!" the girls said in unison.

"I swear you guys are twins. How was your weekend? Mine was full of work."

"We didn't do too much, but our parents are talking about growing a garden."

"Oh no! More pioneers. I'm so sorry. But you could get things like this." Willow pulled out a bag with several hard-boiled eggs and offered one to each.

"Are those eggs?"

"Yep! When was the last time you had one of these?"

Mav started eating hers right away. Reese put hers in the lunch box she carried in her backpack. She carried her backpack everywhere like a security blanket. Also, she didn't like being in the hallways using her locker.

"What are you guys gonna start doing?" Willow asked.

"I have no idea. My parents are talking to my brother about it. They've never done it before and Archer has been watching videos on gardening for days," Maverick said.

"It's a lot of work and it's dirty so be prepared."

"They just argue about it a lot. They don't really include us in it."

"Winter's coming, so there's not much to plant really. Nothing I like anyway. Now's the time to get the soil ready if they don't have anything yet."

"Why are you twirling your hair again?" Mav asked Reese.

"I don't know, I hate talking about it."

"Me too!" Willow interjected, "It's all my parents ever talk about now. Oh wait! By the way..." Willow paused for dramatic effect and tried to hold back a smile. "Guess what I heard."

"What?" Reese and Mav said in unison.

"Jordan Posch has a crush on none other than," Willow twirled her finger in the air and pointed abruptly at Reese with a burst of laughter. Reese instantly turned red and scrunched her face.

"It's totally true, I can tell." Willow continued and laughed.

Maverick could tell her sister was getting overwhelmed, "Okay, that's enough."

Willow stopped and cleared her throat, "Okay, I'm sorry. I think it's adorable though and not a bad—"

"Hey, what elective are you picking?" Mav quickly interrupted to change the subject.

"Archery," Willow answered in a low tone, "My parents of course are making me. Hey Mav! Take it with me! It'll be fun."

Mav didn't care what she took, but they had to pick their electives after the break. Having another class with Willow sounded appealing. The bell rang and they split off to their classes.

***

Archer's day at school was almost over. He walked Evelyn to her math class before heading to his Economics class. "I need to see if we can change our plans this week, I have to work on Thursday. Can we go to dinner Wednesday?" Archer asked.

Evelyn pinched his cheek, "Oh, my man has to work now," she said mockingly. "Yeah, that'll work. Wait, no. I'm going to the recruiter on Wednesday."

"The recruiter? Already?" Archer was a little stunned.

All Evelyn had talked about was joining the Army. She had been talking about it since the day they met. Evelyn wanted to enlist in the Army Corps of Engineers. She constantly talked about 12T, the military occupational specialty for a technical engineer. "I can meet with them now, I'm a senior. I want to get a head start. I need to get a certain score on the ASVAB."

"The what?"

"It's the test you have to take when you enlist. I need a certain score for what I want. We'll talk later, okay?" She kissed him and ducked into her classroom.

Archer jogged in a few seconds late to his last class of the day. He'd started working at Screws and Planks Hardware store the week before. It had only been two eight-hour shifts over the weekend, but he

40

was struggling already to stay focused on school. This was going to be harder than he thought.

He sat next to Miles. He was a good friend. This was the only class they had together this year - U.S. History. He liked the teacher, Mr. Augur, despite what happened the last time he had his class. Archer had taken his World History class as a freshman. He made everything interesting, but graded tough and didn't accept any exceptions or excuses.

It was Monday. Archer completely forgot. He tapped Miles on the shoulder. "I forgot an article."

Miles looked back, "Yeah, I know. That's why I printed one for you." Relief flooded over Archer as Miles offered him a printed sheet of paper and a fist bump. Every Monday, students had to bring an article about the United States. No entertainment news. They had to write their names on it and turn it in. Three unlucky students would be chosen at random to present and discuss their article in front of the class. Archer quickly skimmed the lines on the page and made a wish not to be chosen.

"Good afternoon! Welcome back to your second week. Today is Monday, and you all know what that means." Mr. Augur had a deep voice that echoed through the room. "Do we have any volunteers to present? Of course not. So today, we will be welcoming Vanessa, Charlie, and Braydon." A voice shouted out that Braydon was absent today. Mr. Augur grumbled and looked at his list. "Well then, it looks like Archer will be the stand-in."

Archer grumbled under his breath and tried to read as fast as he could. It was an article about the laundry detergent shortage and how the supply chain had been affected.

Mr. Augur stood up and cleared his podium, "I'm sure nobody is jumping to go first. Let's go in alphabetical order." Archer smiled. He had some time to read. Vanessa's last name was Adams. "Uhm, by first name," Mr. Augur added.

Archer tsked, and his smile vanished.

He strutted up to the front of the class, feigning more confidence than he felt, with a pat on the back from Miles. He held his paper in front of him. Archer stated the title and source of the article, then started to read it to the class. He was interrupted by Mr. Augur and told to use his own words.

"Right, so this is an article about the shortage of laundry detergent, and it explains that there's not really a shortage of the detergent so much as it can't be packaged or get to the stores." There was a deafening silence.

Mr. Augur cleared his throat. "And does the article give any more information about that? Perhaps you could provide your own analysis, Mr. Jenkins."

"Uhm. The wars in Asia and Eastern Europe are the main problem. That's where a lot of our products come from, and there's no way to get them here."

Mr. Augur nodded his head, "Okay, Mr. Jenkins, there's the problem of delivery here in the U.S. as well. Does the article mention anything about that?"

Archer rubbed his chin and put his eyes to the paper in his hand, "Uhm, well. No, I don't—"

"Why can't we just make laundry detergent here?" one of the students interjected. "I just don't get why there's nothing at the store anymore," she continued.

Mr. Augur turned in his seat, looking for where the question came from. "Well, that's a good question. The United States has imported most of its consumer products over the last fifty or so years. That worked really well for a long time to keep prices down. We're trying to shift production now to start producing more goods, but prices are going up dramatically and it will take some time—"

"Take some time?" A voice shouted. It was a face Archer recognized, only by first name, though. His name was Brendon. He'd been in his class since middle school but had never gotten to know him. "And how long do we give them? Meanwhile, people like me are not able to eat. I have an idea, Mr. Augur, how about I read my article?" He uncrumpled a piece of paper and held it above his head. "Why the United States Government Must Be Overthrown." He was starting to shout.

Mr. Augur stood up, "Okay, Brendon—"

"No, Mr. Augur, I think everyone should hear this. Our 'Great Nation' has been all about benefiting the wealthy and exploiting the poor. Now we're all starving and—"

"Brendon, let's scale it back a bit. I appreciate your enthusiasm, but we don't need to shout. Take a deep breath and then continue." Mr. Augur walked over to Brendon, who stood up from his seat.

"Well, that's because I'm upset, and all we seem to hear is just what you said, 'Calm down, it's going to be fine, it's going to get better.' I think that's easy for people like you to say." Brendon stormed out of the class.

The class was silent. Archer awkwardly walked toward his desk and handed his article to Mr. Augar.

***

Stan was sprawled on the coach, watching television. It was on mute. He looked at his phone and reread the two texts he'd received from

Brenda Long at the county asking for an answer about serving on one of the Emergency Management committees. He hadn't responded.

Lexi came downstairs after putting Leo and Blaze to bed. They talked about the grocery store prices and low supply getting worse. She also explained that the credit cards were completely maxed out, and it was time to take another 401 (k) withdrawal. There wasn't much left.

They heard the front door open. Archer slowly strolled in holding his uniform vest, which he tossed on the kitchen table along with his keys.

"Just put your dirty clothes anywhere?" Lexi joked. Archer rolled his eyes but took the vest off the table.

"How was work?" Stan asked.

"It's good. They're really understaffed. Everyone quits, I guess."

"Do you want something to eat?" Lexi asked.

"Yeah, that'd be great!" Archer's eyes lit up.

"Have at it. If you're old enough to make your own decisions, you're old enough to make your own food."

Archer found the jar of almond butter in the pantry. There was no bread, but they had carrots and celery. "Can we please talk about growing some food, you guys? Nobody's down here."

Stan turned the television off. "Alright. Let's talk about it."

"I've been watching a lot of videos. I got a book at the library, and I talked to a couple of people I met at work. I have some ideas on what we can do."

"You went to the library? Never mind. Okay, I got to tell you, your mom and I tried this a long time ago. It was about a year after you were born. We had the same idea. We'd hit a big recession and were strapped for cash. It seriously ended up costing us a ton of money, time, and energy. We ended up with two scrawny cucumbers, a bug-infested skeleton of a tomato and a metric ton of inedible squash. It was a disaster.

We're just not too good with plants," Stan said as Lexi nodded her head the whole time.

"I'd like to try. We'll get Mav and Reese to help. With enough people to spread out the work—"

"Oh, it's going to be all you guys," Lexi interrupted.

Stan shrugged his shoulders. "I'll help. It makes sense. Winter's around the corner, though."

"Exactly!" Archer said, walking over toward the couch with a jar of almond butter. "It's the perfect time to get the ground ready. It's all grass right now, so we can get the soil and beds ready for spring. Plus, we could start composting now."

Stan nodded his head, "We'll need to use a pickaxe to turn over all that grass. It's a lot of work. This red clay out here is tough."

"I found a different method I want to try. You just put cardboard over the grass. Then you put topsoil and mulch over the top. No digging required," Archer said, a little proud of himself and his internet knowledge.

"That doesn't sound very effective. One big rain and it'll wash out I'd think. We should do the tried-and-true method of turning over the soil," Stan retorted.

They continued to discuss and argue about which method would work best. Having had enough, Lexi finally interrupted, "Why not do both? Dad can make his bed, and you can make the one you're talking about. If one fails, hopefully the other works out."

Stan nodded, "I like that. Okay, the backyard is pretty much a perfect square. Probably sixty by forty—"

"It's actually sixty-five by fifty, not counting the ten by thirty along the side of the house. I figure we could put the compost there."

Stan and Archer agreed to start with two side by side beds to try out, leaving plenty of space to complete more if it worked.

"Archer, you're off Wednesday night, right?" Lexi asked with a grin.

"Yeah. Why?"

"Well, you get to come with me to explain this to the HOA."

"The what?" asked Archer.

Stan groaned, "The Homeowners' Association."

Chapter Seven

16 October

14 days before the war

Maverick opened her eyes with a gasp. Archer's face was inches away from hers with a finger over his lips.

"What! What's wrong?" Mav whispered as her heart was racing.

"Come on, get up. I want to show you something. Quiet, though," Archer whispered.

Maverick looked over at Reese, still asleep, holding Leo in her arms. She slowly got up. She was already dressed and just had to put on her shoes.

Archer waited and peered down the hall. He had a big smile on his face. "Come on!" he whispered.

Maverick followed him down the hall as they tiptoed to his room. He opened the window and climbed out. "What are you doing?" Mav whispered sternly.

"Just follow me!" His head disappeared from view. It was barely twilight. Dark purple filled the sky. Mav climbed out of the window, down to the roof of the back porch awning, following Archer's silhouette. Archer dropped down to the ground after dangling for a moment from the edge of the steel awning. Mav walked to the edge and saw Archer below.

"Just do what I did, I'll help you." Mav grabbed the edge with both hands. She felt Archer's arms around her knees, and she let go.

"Alright, come on!" Archer started to jog as they ran through the back alleyway of grass between rows of backyards.

"Where are we going?" Mav whispered.

"Just keep going, you'll see."

Mav realized they were heading toward the river into the woods outside the subdivision. The housing development rested near the bottom of the Appalachian Piedmont. Beyond the river were woods and hills for miles. The kids knew the area pretty well. They would go exploring and hiking a lot when they were younger as well as over the past year.

The sun hadn't risen yet, but there was enough light to see. Archer led her through the trailhead and stopped at the riverbank. They were out of breath and laughing.

"What are we doing here? I don't usually come out here this early. Mom and Dad are gonna be mad."

Archer sat down on a large rock. "Yeah, I know. I left a note." He smiled. Archer stood back up, "Okay, this way." They went off the trail and through brush and branches parallel to the bank. Mist floated on the water, stretching over the bank, making it difficult to see.

They reached a clearing with several large stones that made nearly a perfect circle. "You remember this place?" Archer asked, out of breath.

Maverick scanned around and smiled. "Yeah!" She started to laugh, "I haven't seen this place for years." About six years before, Archer and Mav had several adventures in these woods, and they loved this place. That was before they reached the ages when they were allowed to start using smartphones, which dissolved their adventurous spirits.

"Check this out!" Archer waved her over to a large oak tree. "Remember this?"

Mav looked at the tree trunk and started to laugh. "I can't believe you can still see it!"

On the tree was a large half circle with three smaller circles resembling the shape of a turtle. When Mav first started drawing, her older brother would draw with her. Once she drew a half circle like the shape of a turtle shell. Archer then drew a circle for a head and two circles on the bottom like feet. At five years old, Mav thought this was the funniest thing she'd ever seen. They made this drawing together all the time after that. It stopped about six years ago.

Mav was trying to hold back her tears as she rubbed her fingers over the scar on the tree trunk. "I don't want you to go," her voice cracked as she started to cry.

Archer hugged her tightly. "It's going to be okay."

Archer and Mav sat on the rocks as the sun started to come up. Archer opened his backpack. "When I leave, I want you to be ready. You're the strongest out of all of us."

Mav laughed, "You're funny—"

"I mean it. Mom, Dad, everyone. They all need you. You're the most able to protect everyone. I want to show you something." Archer reached in and withdrew a pistol. It was one of the firearms the family owned. Mav took a deep breath and looked away.

"I know how you're feeling, this is probably the last thing you want to see."

Maverick looked him in the eyes, "I don't think you do know how I feel."

"Okay, that's not what I meant. I just mean, it's important for you to know how to use this, just in case."

"Mom and Dad know about this?"

"No. Forgiveness over permission."

Maverick laughed.

Archer ejected the magazine and locked the slide back, handing it to her. "I'm sorry that happened to you, and I know you're scared. You may need to use one again someday. I want you to be ready."

Maverick held the pistol forward toward the water. Her father had shown her and her sister how to hold it and also the basic rules. Mostly, her parents wanted her and her sister to know what to do if they ever saw a firearm somewhere and how to handle it safely.

Stan had never taught the girls how to shoot firearms. Although Mav had fired the revolver once before, as circumstances had it.

"You're great with the bow. Those skills will help you with this. Aiming is pretty much the same, two sites and making sure your trigger pull is smooth and doesn't mess up your aim." Archer said, loading the magazine.

"All right. I want to try," Maverick said.

Chapter Eight

30 September

395 Days Before the war

The waiting room was standing room only when Stan arrived at the clinic after dropping Blaze off at school. Ruth was arguing with a client about a medication prescription as Stan walked through and unlocked the door into the office area.

Ruth had abruptly halted the conversation through the window, "Stan! Here's the messages from this morning." She handed over a stack of Post-it notes.

His schedule was full of therapy sessions today. The clinic just had another therapist resign for a higher-paying position elsewhere, and their replacement hadn't started yet. His first session for the morning was a long-time client that he'd been working with for several years.

Herbert was a "close to retirement" police officer. That's what he called himself since he'd met with Stan for his initial assessment four years ago. Herbert was in the middle of a contentious divorce and had become extremely depressed and suicidal. The depression had been in remission for more than two years, but Herbert and Stan built a strong rapport, and he chose to keep coming every two weeks. After their usual greeting and check-in, they'd often just have conversations about whatever came up.

Stan couldn't even remember the goals on the treatment plan anymore, but he looked forward to seeing him every couple of weeks.

"Tell me more about the trip." Stan started the session off.

"It was good. Really good. I mean, it was hard too. I haven't changed a diaper in over thirty years. I remember why I hated it so much. At the same time, I loved it. I'm so proud of her." Herbert covered his mouth with his hand and started tearing up. He took a deep breath trying to hold back the tears. "She did everything right. It didn't come from me. They have a beautiful boy. And I don't blame her for not naming him after me. Who wants to be called Herbert?" He laughed.

"What is his name?"

"Ethan."

"That's great," Stan whispered with a big smile.

"I don't like being this far away. I don't blame them for moving. I just wish I was closer."
Herbert sat back in the chair and looked up at the ceiling. "I know I've always talked about retiring and never seem to bring myself to do it. Well, I'm actually gonna do it."

Stan shifted in his seat. "Thinking of moving to Georgia?"

Herbert broke his stare from the ceiling and looked at Stan quizzically, "Hmm? No. I mean, I might, but that's not why."

"Tell me more."

"I've been through my share of tough times. This is the worst. People are struggling. They're angry, and I don't blame them. We're stretched. You know, we don't even respond to a lot of calls anymore. We can't."

"What would it be like for you if you left?"

"I'd be alright. Part of me would feel like a quitter, I think. Part of me wants to run out of the city and head for the hills."

"Or Georgia?"

"Yeah, or Georgia."

"What would it be like for you if you stayed?"

"Well. I don't know. I'm not a big alarmist or anything. You know that. I think it's going to get a lot more violent, though. When that happens, the police have to get more violent. It could just spiral. It's already happening."

***

Twice a week, Mav and Willow had archery class together, which would serve as a PE class over the next quarter. Today was the second class and the first time they got to use the recurve bow. The first class was inside a classroom where they learned about safety on the range, the parts of the bow, as well as arrows, and target scoring. They finished the first class by practicing and demonstrating stringing the recurve bow and figuring out the weight they would start with.

Mav knew nothing about any of this and found it interesting, while Willow seemed busier making jokes and informing everyone that she'd done this before. Mav was nervous. She thought that she'd be unable to pull the string back or that the string or bow would break. That's all she needed, for Willow to see and she'd never hear the end of it.

On the range for the first time, her hand was trembling when she notched the first arrow. The string pulled much easier than she thought it would, and she found she was able to hold it steady. The first shot at twenty yards was high, about six inches in the straw bale above the target, while Willow's hit the outer black ring. Her instructor came over after the first shot and suggested exhaling while sighting and releasing. Her second shot was high in the red ring—much closer. Her instructor said she'd likely need a heavier bow, but to go ahead and keep practicing.

Maverick had a smile on her face and was focused, while Willow had a couple of warnings to stop fooling about. The class, all together, shot around twenty arrows at twenty yards. She was disappointed when it was time to stop and wanted to keep going.

"You're pretty good at that, Robin Hood. My mother would love you." Willow commented as they were putting equipment away. Mav laughed, "I think it's fun, I really like it."

"Do you have a bow?" Willow asked.

"No. I think my brother used to, but I don't know if he still has it."

"You should come over to my house. We have a few different kinds. My dad has a high-powered compound bow he uses to hunt with."

***

Archer convinced Evelyn to leave school early with him to get coffee. She rarely ever skipped class. The same couldn't be said for Archer, he'd often miss lots of classes. Archer drove them over to a small local coffee shop in downtown Gastonia. The Roast Shack was a small coffee roaster that had taken over an old mill building. It was close to the theater where they met and the location of their first date.

"You think you'll be able to turn the entire back yard into a vegetable garden?" Evelyn asked, sipping on her caramel latte. "I mean, your mom says you have trouble taking out the trash."

"I know, I know. This is different. We're having a tough time, and I feel bad for my parents. I don't know much about politics and all that, but people are struggling."

54

Evelyn nodded, "That's true. That's why we're fighting in Europe and Asia. We need the supply chain restored. We need to pull together as a country right now, and it feels like everyone's falling apart. It will get better. I believe in our country."

Archer shrugged, "I hope you're right. I mean, look at the price of gas right now. I know it's not a problem for you, but—"

"What do you mean?"

"I just mean your family has a lot of money, and you guys aren't as bad off."

"It's still bad. We're all in this together."

Archer didn't want to go down this road. He smiled and kissed her. She pulled away with a frown.

"Ah, come on, sweetheart," Archer said, trying to suck up and lay it on thick. Evelyn broke a smile and laughed. "You know you could always help."

Evelyn cocked her head, "help with what?"

"Help us with the garden, Ms. Army Corps of Engineers. Or does my princess not want to get her hands dirty?"

Evelyn swatted Archer's hand, "You better watch it. Sure, I'll help, but that means more time around your mom. She always looks at me. Like she thinks I'm up to no good."

Archer nearly spit out his drink, "My mom loves you, what are you talking about? She just wishes you were her child instead of me, is all."

***

After dinner, the Jenkins family had taken a short car ride to the community center in town where the open, quarterly HOA meeting was being held. Lexi joked in the van that this would be the most people they've likely ever had at a meeting when the van unloaded. She'd gone to most of the meetings since she stopped working. It helped to get her mind off just watching and worrying about the kids.

To her surprise, the lot was full, and they had to park far down the road on the side of the street. As they endured Leo and Blaze's grumbling about how long the walk was, they approached the glass entry doors. Through the windows, they could see it was standing room only. They slowly staggered in. The meeting hadn't started yet, and the volume was loud with chatter. They saw a few people they recognized, but most of them, they didn't.

Stan stood close to Lexi and leaned over toward her ear, "You think you'll be able to bring up the gardening?"

Lexi shrugged her shoulders, "It's never been like this. It's usually me and a few others at most. They always kept it informal. I have no idea what they'll do with this."

A woman stepped up in front of the table where the board members sat. "Hi everyone! Everyone! Please!" She was able to get everyone to quiet down easily. She introduced herself as the coordinator from the property management company that managed the HOA services. She didn't live in the development. She explained the process of the open meeting and that the turnout was very unexpected. She explained that open meetings were for members to bring up and discuss issues, but nothing would be voted on or changed today.

"We'll try to take as many comments or questions as we can in the next hour. Please try to be as quick and concise as possible to give everyone a turn."

Usually, the business in the meetings was focused on complaints around unsightly yards and ways to enforce the rules. Debate around how much authority the HOA should or shouldn't have was always brought up. This meeting was different. For most, this was their first meeting. The tension was high.

One by one, residents brought up the rules and regulations around gardening. Most were already using their backyards, and they wanted to use the front yard as well. Break-ins around the neighborhood were another issue brought up.

"We need a neighborhood watch!" Bob stood up boldly and faced the residents. He purposely and dramatically turned his back toward the panel. Lexi remembered Bob's quick temper from six months ago when he yelled at the board for their incompetence on handling the parking on the streets.

He proceeded to describe a break-in at his home. "They busted out a window and came right in. It was two in the morning. They didn't care that we were home. They were grabbing food out of the pantry and going through my fridge. I chased them out with my shotgun." Bob was trying to keep his voice and demeanor calm as his wife started to nudge his shoulder, keeping him on track. Bob said he called 9-1-1, and nobody came to the house. Since the perpetrators were gone and nobody was injured, law enforcement never arrived. He was given a phone number to call and make a report. A number of the residents in the crowd gave supportive praises and cheers as Bob continued to talk. He was finally cut off after exceeding his time.

Stan was trying to wrangle Blaze and keep him still in front of him. They were getting restless as the residents continued, one by one, expressing their challenges and proposed solutions. Stan lightly pinched Lexi's arm to get her attention. She shrugged it off, staying focused on the speaker. Stan shuddered and took a deep breath as the realization hit him. He knew his wife well. He may have been the social worker by education and profession, but Lexi was the social worker through spirit and practice. Two years ago, she was focused on ensuring the kids in her class had breakfast, then the whole school, then the county and the state. Three years ago, it was access to medical care. When Lexi was convinced of a complex problem and a need that many others were suffering from, she'd get locked in. Stan could tell in that moment that this was it. Her view was going to change. Which meant his view would have to change.

A woman with her children standing in front of her was speaking to the crowd. Stan missed what she was saying, but she was wiping tears and trying to keep her composure. Lexi marched up through the tight rows of crowded seats toward her. She stood next to her and put an arm around her shoulder. Lexi had completely skipped over the line behind her and confidently waved off the coordinator who was about to interrupt.

"Hi everyone, I'm Lexi Jenkins. It's good to see everyone here tonight. I have to say, I was coming tonight to ask the board about the rules on gardening, thinking I'd be the only one. I just had no idea. I'll admit, I've been in some denial. I've wanted to believe everything was going to get better or return to normal. I just had no idea about how much of an impact everything has had on everyone else. I don't think things are going to get better the way I hoped. I don't think anyone is coming to our rescue. So, we need to help ourselves. We are a community, and I think we should all get to know each other and start working together. I'll tell you all that sitting here, I'm thinking it's time to find solutions—growing our own food, helping keep our neighborhood safe and secure."

Applause and cheers started to sound off in the room as she finished her speech. Lexi met and shook hands with as many neighbors as she could and exchanged contact information to start a large group chat.

The Jenkins family was the last to leave the meeting as they slowly shuffled out to the car. Stan looked over at his wife and grinned as they reached it. She rolled her eyes at him, "Yeah, yeah, I know."

On the short trip home, Stan pulled out his phone and sent a text to Brenda at the county.

If the committee still has an opening, I'm interested.

Chapter Nine

17 October

13 days before the war

Stan sat in his seat staring at the white board cluttered with black hand-drawn boxes, letters, numbers, and arrows. He tried to soften his gaze and lose focus on the shouting around him at the table. Brenda pounded the cheap particleboard conference table, trying to restore order in the room. When the room finally went silent, Brenda pointed at Edwin Daas to continue.

Edwin was in his mid-twenties. He flashed an artificial confidence in his job—lots of knowledge but little experience. Stan struggled to take him seriously. Edwin represented a unified voice of local law enforcement, which included three county sheriff departments and police departments of the local townships and cities within the counties.

Edwin held out a hand and took a breath to calm himself down. "Nearly all of our resources are utilized just to keep food, water, and power distributed, and keep order to prevent riots. These draft notices are resulting in a huge backlash that we cannot respond to right now— "

"How can we even have a draft? Who are we at war with?" A voice interrupted.

"Where's the national guard?" another shouted as the grumbling and arguments revived.

"Please! Everyone," Brenda shouted, jumping back on her feet. "We can't fall apart like this."

Stan groaned and put his hand to his forehead. It felt hopeless. All the reasons he hated committees came flooding back. He didn't want to start talking. He knew he'd just get angry like everyone else. It was useless.

Brenda let out a deep sigh and slouched her shoulders. "Here's what we're going to do. Mr. Fredrickson has come a long way to meet with us today. As I mentioned, he's here from Washington to inform us on what's going on. He's a messenger. Please, everyone, just listen and compose yourselves so we can get through this."

Mr. Fredrickson seemed unfazed. He gave a professional grin and nod. "Thank you, Ms. Long. Everyone, please. I understand this is a crisis. We are trying to maintain order. Not just here in the county, but at the state and federal levels. From my understanding, the draft is a response to maintain that order. I don't have details on how the military will be utilized. We need to ensure the security of our nation."

Stan rolled his eyes. Brenda noticed and shot a glare.

"I know you all have a lot of questions, and my role here today is to document those questions and return with answers." Audible groans followed. "In addition to that," Mr. Fredrickson raised his voice to interrupt and continue, "I am looking for any information and complaints about any organized local activity which my counterpart here, agent Sorenson, will be taking care of." The room was eerily silent.

"You'll have to forgive us, Mr. Fredrickson, and I believe I'm speaking for everyone here. We're all a bit weary and confused." Stan calmy interjected through the silence.

"Confused about what? Mr. ..."

"Jenkins. Many of our own children have received these draft notices. I hope you appreciate how concerning this is. No time in history has there ever been a draft when we're not at war."

"There have been peacetime drafts."

"Sure, but there was a known reason why. We don't know anything about what's going on. We have a ton of information from the internet. An endless supply of information telling us everything and nothing all at once. There's no official word anymore, and when there is, we all hear it's fake. We've heard it all. The government has already collapsed, we're being invaded by foreign countries. We've heard that several states have seceded. We've heard of revolution in the northwest. Some say military units have attempted a coup. It's this group, that group—"

"Mr. Jenkins, I understand your—"

"No! I don't think you do, Mr. Fredrickson. I can't really understand why you're here talking to us and who this agent is with you. We're just an advisory committee for a rural county."

Brenda firmly put her hand over Stan's and whispered for him to stop. She then turned her attention to the group, "I think we should end the meeting here, everyone. Some of you are going to be contacted individually, just keep your phones close."

As everyone slowly stood up, Brenda motioned for Stan to follow her. Stan's eyes were welling up. He wanted to scream and throw something heavy. He followed Brenda into an empty office and closed the door behind him.

"I can't imagine what you're feeling right now. I'm not going to pretend to. But I need you to take a pause and try to calm yourself."

"I just don't understand who they are and why they're here. Someone from the federal government speaking to us about the draft by just taking questions and disappearing? Is that how that works?"

"I don't know. I just want you to be careful. I don't have a good feeling."

"What are you saying?"

"I don't know. I can't really say for certain. I'm just getting more and more silence from above." *Brenda took a deep breath and forced a smile.* *"When does Archer leave?"*

Stan looked down at the floor and brushed his fingers through his hair, "Twelve days. Brenda, what's wrong? Why'd you stop the meeting?"

Brenda paused thoughtfully, "I think they're here to question us."

Chapter Ten

12 October

383 Days before the war

Light was barely coming through the windows when Stan opened the blinds in the girls room at 6:30 a.m.

"Noooo, it's Saturday!" Reese whined, covering her face with her pillow.

"Let's go! It's gonna be a busy day," Stan chirped as he pulled Maverick's foot toward the floor.

Stan and Lexi had a tougher time getting Archer out of bed about fifteen minutes earlier. He was exhausted from work the previous day. This was the first free weekend day the family had since the HOA meeting, and Lexi had spent the last few days thinking, researching, and planning. She informed Stan last night that things were going to change starting today.

Archer's eyes were barely open as he robotically cracked eggs into a large bowl downstairs in the kitchen. Mav and Reese came downstairs to see Blaze and Leo sitting at the table, arguing over how to correctly eat raisins. Lexi had pulled what appeared to be an odd-shaped loaf of bread or cake from the oven as Archer paused to study it.

"What? It's oatmeal bread. We have to get a little creative now. And don't use all the eggs!" she snapped.

Stan yawned and raised his arms up to the ceiling as he plopped down into his seat at the kitchen table. Mav snatched the bowl of raisins and dumped them into her mouth. Blaze and Leo protested.

"Why are we up so early?" Maverick asked with her mouth full.

"We have a lot to do today, and we need a family meeting to talk about some changes," Lexi answered as she was doing several things at once with urgency. Stan couldn't help but run through the symptoms of mania in his mind while watching her. She'd been like this before, and it usually would fizzle out. He just let her have her time to get her energy out.

"What do you mean? What needs to change?" Reese asked, starting to twirl her hair.

Lexi started to cut the loaf into several slices. "We need to make some changes to how we live. *We* are going to have more responsibility than what we're used to. So, I want us to talk about that and answer any questions you all may have."

Everyone was silent. Stan could tell this was resulting in more questions and worry than answers.

He interjected, "Well, some changes, yeah. But it's all stuff that will make us stronger and more ready to be grown-ups. Face the world, you know? You're all getting older and closer to being adults, and we need to make sure we learn to take care of ourselves." Stan watched Archer leaning his head back balancing several raisins on his forehead, completely ignoring the eggs he'd left on the stove.

Reese and Mav exchanged confused looks. Stan put his hand on Lexi's shoulder, "Okay, okay. Sweetheart, how about we just leave breakfast to Archer? He's got this. Come over and have a seat."

Lexi took a deep breath and glared at Stan who flashed a cheesy grin back at her. She walked over and sat at the table. She smiled at the kids who all stared at her expectantly.

"Did someone die or something?" Mav asked.

Archer let out a frustrated groan, "What's the big deal? Listen, everyone, food is too expensive, and we need to grow some vegetables in the backyard and sell some stuff—"

"Archer!" Lexi shouted, cutting him off.

"Yes, thank you for your help, Archer," Stan sarcastically added.

"I knew it, we're gonna starve. We're gonna be like Willow's family." Reese whined.

"Are we gonna starve?" Blaze shouted.

Lexi rolled her eyes. "We are not going to starve."

"I knew about everything costing a lot. How is growing vegetables going to feed us all? What do we do about meat and bread?" Mav asked.

"Well, growing some food will help, and I've been talking with a lot of the neighbors who are all doing the same thing. If we can all work together, share, and trade, it could actually help a lot. It can really save us a ton of money, which… would really help right now. There are other things we can do, too."

"Like what?" Reese said, squirming in her seat.

"Well, we can work together with our neighbors. Some of them are raising chickens or trying to. We could maybe do some work and help them if they need it, then they may be willing to help us if we need it. We can trade with them to maybe get eggs and other things. We'll make sure not to waste anything. We can look at all the clothes we have, all the old ones that don't fit and see if anyone needs them and they'll do the same."

"We have boxes and boxes of clothes that your mother was supposed to donate but they just sit. And sit—"

"Thanks, Stan. I think we know." Lexi quipped. She continued to ramble her plan and was starting to speed up her words. Stan could tell. When Lexi was focused on a project, she had superhuman strength. It came at a cost, though.

Stan tried to find a smooth way to interrupt. "Maybe, we can break this down into what we want everyone to do, step by step?"

Breakfast was tense when it started, but as they discussed what they wanted to do, the kids started to get excited. They made a plan for the day to start making two garden beds in the backyard. Reese and Mav were excited to try using the pickaxe, shovel, and trowel. They'd seen them in the garage before, but never actually used them.

Mav had texted Willow to let her know what they were starting today and told her parents that Willow and her family could be a big help.

Stan and Lexi asked Archer about seeds and transplants. Archer explained that seeds were sold quickly, and they rarely remained in stock for more than a day. He had been talking to many of the regular customers who had been practicing horticulture on their properties, which he had been trying to learn more about. Archer said that he would talk to the manager and see if he could purchase seeds at the next delivery before they went on the shelves.

Archer had been talking to others in the area and reading about what grows well with the clay they have in the backyard. Lexi had made a group chat with twelve other residents in the neighborhood and created a spreadsheet of who was growing what. The numbers joining the group chat were increasing every day.

The following week was exhausting for everyone. They'd work for several hours in the early morning and evening on weekend days to avoid the lingering heat of early fall. It was muddy and painful and almost didn't feel right to see the grass lawn ripped apart. Everyone's hands were sore and blistered. Despite his ego, Stan agreed that plowing by hand with a pickaxe was far too much. Archer was able to rent a gas-powered tiller from Screws and Planks at a discount which made the process much easier. The work was intense and tiring for everyone. It wasn't perfect by any means, but over several days, the family forged a togetherness that life before never had.

Stan realized how out of shape he'd become after the first hour of this project. He and Archer argued several times about the process and how to properly use the tools. Even after just a week, they'd produced two beds covered with mulch. Fall was days away. While everyone, even Leo and Blaze, had helped with the gardening, Lexi and the girls were going through the garage and finding items to use, sell, or trade. With help from neighbors, the residents set up a private social media account for the neighborhood to post items needed, items to sell, and requests for services.

Lexi had unboxed her sewing machine that had, at one time, been a brief passion of hers. Reese was extremely interested and had started to learn basic sewing skills very quickly. Lexi and Reese were preparing and planning to repair old clothes they could collect and upcycle, clothing, blankets, towels, etc., from neighbors.

After many hours of discussion over a few days, Stan had gone into the safe and pulled out his firearm collection, which he hadn't used in over ten years. Stan, in his youth and early adult years, had enjoyed collecting and shooting firearms. He never hunted once in his life and didn't have a desire to, but hearing about all the break-ins that were happening at least once or twice per week in the neighborhood, he was increasingly concerned. He had no plans to just leave them lying about but thought it wouldn't be a bad idea to keep them ready.

Stan had sold most of his firearms over the years and only had three left: a .357 revolver, a 9mm pistol and 12-gauge shotgun. He showed his collection to Archer, and they spent a couple of hours on a Sunday night cleaning and lubricating them. Archer said he remembered shooting all three of them when he was about ten years old but couldn't remember much about them.

Lexi had agreed that they would keep the revolver ready. Stan would keep the others in the safe but would put the revolver in the bedroom. They had a crash safety course for all the kids and had them hold it, open the cylinder and so on. They decided it would be best that the kids all knew where it was, and they trusted that they were all obedient enough to leave it alone and be safe with it around.

As the home became more organized, Stan and Lexi's overall anxiety started to drop and their sense of competence and control was starting to slowly grow.

Chapter Eleven

18 October

12 days before the war

Reese was turning the compost pile before anyone else was up. Her hoodie was a little too snug as she had grown out of it easily last year. She paused to catch her breath, noticing the frost in the air.

"Why are you up so early?"

Reese startled and dropped the pitchfork to the ground. She turned around to see Mav in the doorway. Her arms were folded, and she shivered with a grimace on her face.

"I'm always up early. Why are you up so late?" Reese responded as she reached down and snatched the tool off the ground.

"What's wrong?"

"We have lots of work to do."

"I'll help you—"

"No, I'm fine." Reese snapped. "Why don't you just take off like you usually do and leave me to do all the work around here." Reese continued to turn the pile with fervor. Maverick could hear her sister sniffle as she was attempting to hide her tears. Maverick was puzzled. Her sister was rarely mad at her or didn't show it if she was.

Maverick stepped into the cold and squeezed her crossed arms tighter around herself.

"What's the matter, Reese?" Reese ignored her. "What did I do wrong? Look, Archer's going to be okay—."

"No! It's Nothing." Reese was just stabbing the compost pile and finally tossed the handle down to the ground. She made an about-face and folded her arms, giving Maverick a death stare. She was breathing heavily. "It's not just Archer. It's you. You already left!"

Mav continued to stare, dumbfounded, "What do you mean?"

"Ever since that night. You haven't been the same. It's like you're not my sister, and it's only getting worse. You run out into the woods every day before anyone gets up."

Mav dropped her head. Reese's words made her heart start pounding inside. She was trying to think of words to say but couldn't get them past the lump in her throat.

"You know it's true," Reese continued, "I don't even know who you are anymore."

Archer suddenly poked his head out of the doorway. "Good morning, guys. Wow, Mav, you're still here. Gonna help out today?"

Mav huffed, "I do lots of work around here. I don't see anyone else bringing meat home. You're welcome."

Archer shrugged, "You go out a lot to get meat, but don't necessarily bring lots back. Lucky for us, we've got Reese here," he said with a sly wink.

Mav shook her head, clearly annoyed. "Why are you up so early?" she asked, trying to change the subject.

Archer chugged the glass of water he was holding. After a burp, he said, "We're going to see if there's any mail."

Mail delivery was infrequent and would often collect at the local substation for pickup. Most of the mail they received was several weeks old with the exception of the draft notice Archer received, which was very timely.

About an hour later, Archer and Stan were outside the local post office and waited in line to see what undelivered mail they'd received. Archer had only received one letter from Evelyn and that was while she was in boot camp. She'd enlisted and left for boot camp in July. Archer had not talked to her since. Archer had talked to Evelyn's parents, who said they hadn't been able to reach her by phone either and that cell phones were apparently restricted.

Stan shuffled through a small stack of envelopes he received at the counter. He withdrew a small envelope and held it up. Archer snatched it from his hand. It was from Evelyn. It was postmarked over 5 weeks ago. Oddly, the letter came from Fort Benning, Georgia and not Missouri where 12T training was held.

Dear Archer,

I love you and miss you so much. I am sorry I have not been able to call you. So much has happened. The day before boot camp graduation, I was told that my MOS was administratively changed from 12T to 11B. That means that I am no longer going to be an engineering specialist. I've been redesignated for infantry. They said that's what they needed right now. I'm really upset by this, but I will do what is needed. At any rate, I have been sent to Fort Benning in Georgia rather than Fort Leonard Wood in Missouri. The training is usually 22 weeks, but it's been reduced to 16 because we're needed on deployment. They won't let us have cell phones here, and we are restricted from leaving most of the time.

All we ever hear are rumors. We hear we're being deployed to Texas or somewhere northwest to protect our nuclear arsenal. I have no idea what's going to happen, and I am scared. There are rumors of insurgency all over the country. Some states are talking of secession. I've met a ton of others here who were once deployed overseas, and now they are being redeployed all over the country. I'm afraid a civil war is imminent.

I miss home very much. I miss you most of all. I think I made a mistake. I wish we could be together right now. I love you. I hope my letters are getting to you. I send you a letter at least once a week, but I haven't gotten a response from you. A few times I've had access to a phone, and I can't get through because the network is busy. Please stay safe and know that I love you.

Love,
Evelyn

Stan was watching Archer read it, taking his eyes off the road for much too long. "Well, what'd she say?"

Chapter Twelve

26 October

369 Days before the war

Weekends became the busiest days for the family in the last month. Every morning, the kids woke up to a long, exhausting list of chores mostly in the backyard. Archer was no exception, even though he had to be at work by 8:00 a.m. to open the store, alongside Miles.

Saturday mornings became an informal meeting time at Screws and Planks where a few of the locals would meet in the outdoor garden in the rear of the building. Along the rows of mulch, several old men would gather and drink coffee, chatting about their homestead projects. Miles would often sit in and chat. Archer didn't think much of it. Miles had been working at the store longer, and they were more familiar with him, but whenever Archer came by, the men seemed to hush and wait for him to pass. Maybe it was just in his head.

"Archer!" Miles shouted across the empty store. Archer looked over and saw Miles waving his hand to come over to the group. Archer felt a rushing awkwardness hit him suddenly as he rose up from his knees where he was facing shelves of red clay containers. He approached the group sitting on sacks of mulch. They were old-looking. Rough. Half of them peered at him and the rest just looked away.

"Guys, this is Archer. He's my best friend. I've known him a long time," Archer almost flinched at the title Miles gave their friendship. Sure, they were friends. Best friends? Archer got the sense that Miles was trying to help these gentlemen feel at ease.

"Hey guys," Archer blurted out with a raised hand and awkward smile. The men didn't acknowledge. The silence made Archer hope for the ground to open so he could be swallowed up and this could be over.

"Hi Archer!" One of the men who was looking at him and smiling finally said. He had the face of a catcher's mitt but had kind blue eyes. "How do you like your job here at the old Planks?"

Archer started to breathe again. "It's great!" I'm learning a lot. I'm trying to learn more about growing fruits and vegetables. That's why I'm here. Well, besides being with my best friend here." Archer let out a chuckle.

The man nodded and smiled. His eyes pierced through him. "I think that's a wise choice, young man. How is the journey so far?"

Archer was nervous, but he was also frustrated with some of the problems he and his father were running into. He explained what they had tried and what their goals were.

"That won't work!" One of the men exclaimed. So far, Archer had only been talking to the catcher's mitt with piercing blue eyes. One of the men who seemed to be ignoring Archer's presence interjected. "This here is red clay. It needs nitrogen. In the olden days, you could add stuff to the soil. Just do what you can grow. Sounds like it's peppers and squash. Just stick with that." All the men interjected. Some agreed, some started to argue. "You need lime! Wood ash can work too." Another yelled out that it would be too much work for all that.

Archer was overwhelmed. He realized this is what would really help him, though. Miles peered at him with a sly grin and a wink. This went on for several minutes as the men all engaged in deep discourse.

The catcher's mitt man stood up and walked to Archer's side. "I'm Calvin. Calvin Eastridge. It's nice to meet you, Archer." Calvin held out his hand and Archer shook it. Calvin had a tight grip and shake that jarred Archer to his core. He shook Archer's hand.

Archer couldn't help but smile. "Thank you, Mr. Eastridge. It's good to meet you, too."

Mr. Eastridge nodded. "I bet working here will be helpful. You get to learn about all the tools of the trade and such. I don't get to come in much anymore. I've been traveling all about lately."

"Yes, sir. That's the very reason I wanted to come work here. I do get a discount, too."

"These boys meet here every Saturday morning as I'm sure you've seen. I used to, but now just come by when I can. I know this can look like a grumpy bunch, but they would love to help. Self-sufficiency should be our top priority right now, and I want to commend you for setting out on that journey."

Archer smiled, "Thank you, again, Mr. Eastridge."

***

After nearly three to four weeks of rescheduling and delays, the first LEPC subcommittee meeting was underway. Stan was not very excited to be part of this, especially on a weekend—however, he really wanted to know what in the world was going on in the community.

Maybe he'd get answers, but he was very skeptical. Committees were rarely productive in his experience. Stan sat in front of a large oval table at the county building he once worked at. It brought back memories. He didn't recognize any faces but recognized a few names. Sixteen members sat at the table, talking amongst themselves. Brenda was at the head of the table, writing a note and checking her watch.

Brenda rose from her chair. Still writing a note. "Thank you, everyone." Her voice hushed the table. "I want to thank you all for your service today and in the upcoming weeks and months." The silence remained. Stan leaned back in his chair and let out a sigh. 'Upcoming months' did not sound good to him at all.

"I'd like to start by explaining the mission of this committee. You will be hearing some information here that is very important and vital to our community. I want to be sure that everyone is very serious about the need for confidentiality, as I've discussed with all of you personally." Brenda scanned the table. Everyone's eyes were on hers except Stan's. Brenda shuffled her planner and paused. She seemed distracted by the notes she had likely rehearsed previously. Brenda walked over to the wall which was a giant whiteboard from floor to ceiling. She pulled a cap off a black marker and started to draw several boxes with acronyms inside. She drew lines connecting each of the boxes. Stan's mouth hung open with a face of agony. He closed his eyes, rubbing his forehead with his fingertips. He started to question his decision.

When she finished drawing, she capped the marker and stood tapping on a box in the center. "This is us. We are an ad hoc advisory subcommittee to the Local Emergency Planning Committee for Gaston County. We will receive action bulletins that will need to be implemented by the LEPC. We review the bulletins first and discuss how we think these changes will affect the community and give any guidance we can suggest for smooth rollout given how close all of you are to the community." This was Brenda's strength. She paused and noticed a hand raised, and it seemed to disturb her flow. "Yes, Roger?"

Stan had seen Roger once before. He did something with the schools and Stan couldn't remember his last name. He didn't even remember his first name until Brenda said it.

Roger cleared his throat. "Are we voting on these changes or recommending how the committee votes?"

Brenda shook her head as soon as he said the word vote and just waited for his words to stop. "These are not being voted on. These are orders."

Roger looked perplexed, "Orders from who or where?"

Brenda quickly replied, "The state and federal government. I'm not sure of the system in place or how they're made, but I know they're mandated changes we must follow. We're simply providing our opinion and analysis to the LEPC on how we feel these will be accepted by the people in the county. We also give any suggestions to accommodate those changes based on the needs of the community."

Brenda continued to draw connecting lines between police departments, private security companies, the Sheriff's department and so on. She explained they would work directly with distributors from the state and federal government to provide supplies and groceries to local grocery stores. She stated one of the first and most important directives to review would be creating a schedule for community members to visit grocery stores at scheduled times, provide suggestions on communication to the community and work with the stores to manage limits on products.

Stan would feel bored any other time, but he couldn't believe what he was hearing. "When is this happening, Brenda?"

Brenda stood in front of the wall with scrawled lines and boxes. She capped the dry-erase marker. "Very soon."

***

Mav and Reese were standing at the door when Archer walked in after a long day of work. They stared at him expectantly.

"What?" He whined as the feeling hit him that his mother needed him to do something for them.

Lexi yelled through the kitchen, "I need you to take them to their friend's house, I can't do it right now." Blaze was crying in the kitchen as Lexi was trying to get him to remove an old band-aid.

"Awe, Mom! I have to—"

"Don't start, Archer! That's my car you're driving, and if you think—"

"Alright, alright!" He interrupted. Archer dropped his shoulders and made an about-face toward the door. "Come on, let's go."

"Wait!" Lexi stormed into the living room while Blaze continued to wail—Leo joined in and started to cry out of sympathy. "Hey, I haven't met these people before. I texted them, but I want you to walk them to the door and meet the parents."

Archer dropped his head and sighed.

"Don't give me that! Just say 'hi' and make sure the people aren't crazy or dangerous."

Archer followed the GPS on his phone to Willow's house. It was a quiet ride, and Archer was still fuming. He wanted to go home and take a nap. He was still getting used to hours standing on his feet. The house was in a rural community with only two or three neighbors in sight. The house was a modular home and shaped like a shoe box. The siding was possibly white but covered in green and black mold. Contrasting the filthy exterior was a clean white sign that stated, 'NO SOLICITORS.' The house wasn't very large, but there were a lot of trees and brush in the front and sides. There were several cars that likely didn't run in the driveway by the looks of the dust and dirt that faded out their original colors.

"Who are these people?" Archer asked, feeling skeptical.

"Willow," both the girls said in unison.

"Does Willow wear shoes by chance?" Archer asked with a grin, but the girls didn't seem to understand the joke.

Archer, Mav, and Reese walked up to the door. Archer softly knocked, releasing an explosion of dogs barking from within the house and around the property. Reese started to bite her lip and twirl her hair.

"Stop it," Maverick snapped with a whisper as Reese dropped her hand to her side. They could hear voices scolding dogs inside.

Within seconds, the front door flew open. Willow stood with a big smile, "Hey, you guys are here—" Willow interrupted herself when she caught sight of Archer, "Oh, well hello," she said in a soothing voice and big smile.

Maverick rolled her eyes.

"Come on in, guys," Willow waved them in and shouted for her mom and dad.

Willow's parents entered the room. They were covered in sweat and red clay. "Hi there," Willow's mother said in an inviting and endearing tone. Willow's father spoke in a short tone with a big smile and a hearty nod.

"Mom, this is Maverick, Goose and—Iceman?" Willow joked as the parents nodded in confusion.

Archer bellowed a laugh. He thought that was extremely funny. Mav and Reese remained unfazed.

"Hi, I'm Archer, I'm their brother. My mom couldn't bring them over, so I'm here to drop them off." Archer held out his hand and greeted both parents, who were extremely friendly. Willow grabbed Mav and Reese by the arm and whisked them away to her bedroom. Archer looked out the back window and noticed sprawling garden beds with lush green vegetation in the backyard. "Hey, that's an amazing garden!"

***

Willow led Mav and Reese into her room. It was quite different from the rest of the house.

"Wow, you like pink," Maverick said with a chuckle.

Willow let out a groan, "I know, I know, I'm going to repaint it. This was the room I got, and a five-year-old princess cousin of mine was here long ago, I think. We just moved in here recently, remember?"

Maverick chuckled as Reese looked around the pink walls, "I like it." Maverick noticed a compound bow hanging on the wall adjacent to the bedroom door. "Oh, is that the bow you were telling me about? Can I see it?"

Willow pulled her bow from the wall and started to show her how it worked and how it was different from the recurves they had used in class. Reese was looking at small figurines on Willow's dresser.

"Oh, Reese, did you finally notice how Jordan looks at you? I keep hearing about it."

Reese shook her head and kept looking at the dresser. "Oh, come on, he's super cute. You should just try to talk—"

"Can I use your bathroom?" Reese interrupted. She was biting her lip, and her face was flushed and spotty red.

"Yeah, sure. Two doors to the left."

Reese quickly exited the room and went into the bathroom.

"I don't get it, what's up with your sister?"

Maverick was tugging the string and eyeing the sight on the compound bow. "She gets super anxious, especially when it comes to boys."

"Why, though?"

"Last year at our old school, she had been told that a boy liked her. Kayden. That's his name. He actually lives in our neighborhood. Anyway, it got around and Ashley McFarland, the 6th grade beauty queen got jealous or something. She started to make things up about Reese and pick on her. That's around the time her acne got bad, too. One day, Ashley called her Retin-A instead of Renee. The whole class laughed at her, and the name stuck. She wouldn't go to school for a week after that. Then she changed her name to Reese."

Willow stared through the wall toward the bathroom as if she could see Reese sitting in there. "Oh, that sucks."

Mav tried to release an arrow from the quiver but couldn't figure out how to release it. "Well, the whole changing her name thing, my parents were trying to talk her out of it. My dad said she had to face it and changing her name would just make them win. It didn't matter. She wasn't changing her mind, and my parents were just making it worse. I tried to get them to leave her alone and they wouldn't. So, I changed my name, too. That made them pretty mad, but it got them off her back. I don't get too bothered when our parents are mad at me."

"Huh!" Willow was impressed.

"I guess I was just being supportive, but now I like it. The best part though was the last day of the school year. The middle school got out early and I was able to walk over to the elementary school just as they all got out to go home. I found Ashley and pushed her hard. She fell over a bench and I think got a concussion. I got in a lot of trouble for that, but it was worth it."

"Nice!" Willow snapped the release to free the arrow. Mav held the bladed tip of the arrow in the light.

"I think Renee is a beautiful name. That's a shame. What's your real name?"

Mav finally looked Willow in the eye, "Mavis."

Willow pressed her finger to her chin and gave a thoughtful look, "Huh… I think Maverick's a good name."

***

Reese stared at her face in the mirror. She leaned close to the mirror, counting the zits on her forehead and rubbing them. She stared at her reflection and shook her head. She took several deep breaths and closed her eyes, counting backward from ten. She felt her stomach churning and a lump in her throat. She didn't want to go back. She decided to see if Archer had left yet so maybe she could go back with him. She entered the empty living room and could see Archer and Willow's parents talking in the backyard in front of the massive rows of garden beds. Reese was in awe. All the different vegetables looked amazing to her. She completely forgot about the ensuing panic attack. She slid the glass door open and walked out to the wooden deck where Archer and the parents were talking.

"Oh, hi sweetheart, everything alright?" Willow's mother asked.

Reese smiled as she smelled the soil and floral scents hit her nose. "This is so beautiful," Reese said. She had thoughts of running through the neatly tilled rows.

Willow's father smiled, "Why, thank you. I was just telling your brother here what we're up to. Sounds like you guys are getting into this yourselves." Reese smiled and nodded her head. He continued, "Why don't you come on over? I was just showing your brother how to grow potatoes in straw. It's easy. You can do it anytime, anywhere."

Through the afternoon, Willow's parents were showing how they now mostly use a 'no-till' method for most of their beds. He explained that while they used wooden planks as borders for the beds, it wasn't necessary. That was mostly for neatness and keeping the mud under control, especially when it rained.

Mav and Willow came out as well and were able to practice using the bow. Willow's father was helpful to Mav in learning the compound bow, which she took to rather easily after she'd had some use with the recurve.

Later that evening, the three of them returned home. Lexi was surprised that Archer had stayed the whole time but was excited to hear about Willow's parents and the skills they had. She was, however, rather upset when she learned that they would be coming for dinner next weekend without knowing first.

"Forgiveness over permission," Archer reminded Mav when his mother was done yelling at him that night.

Chapter Thirteen

19 October

11 days before the war

Archer had arrived at the Food Towne USA over 20 minutes before it opened. Since he was over sixteen years old, he was able to buy groceries on his own and was considered an adult for his household. The county had provided a roster for over the last 4 months that allowed grocery shopping every two weeks at designated stores based on zip code. You had a six-hour window to complete your shopping, or else you had to wait for the next two weeks.

The grocery stores were relatively safe and heavily guarded by police and mostly private security hired by the county. Stan and Lexi felt safe sending Archer on his own. He also needed something to do since Screws and Planks closed down a few weeks ago and he no longer had a job. The line wrapped around the back of the store. It was the best time before everything got purchased.

"Archer!" It was Miles. They arranged to meet up as they both coincidentally had the same grocery window. Miles jogged over and joined him in line.

"Where's your mom?" Archer asked.

"It's just me, she doesn't leave the house anymore."

"I get that."

"How many days you got left?"

Archer shot Miles a look, "Eleven. What about you?"

Miles paused. He glanced over his shoulder. "Come on. You know I ain't doing any of that."

"Yeah, I know. I think you should, though."

"I can't."

"Yes, you can. You just don't—" Archer cut himself off as he looked down at Miles who exposed his forearm by pulling back his sleeve, revealing a fresh tattoo of an upside-down three-point crown in a circle.

Archer huffed and shook his head. "Are you crazy?"

"Are you?" Miles shot back. "Dude, look around you. Look what's happening to us. You want to enlist and fight to keep us living like this? Get killed for nothing? Don't you think it's time for a change?"

Archer scanned around the line nervously. It didn't appear anyone was listening. He whispered close in Miles' ear, "You know you could end up disappearing with that thing on your arm, someday."

Miles leaned his back away and smiled. "I don't care anymore." His eyes were welling up as he was fighting to keep his smile on his face.

Archer's head dropped, looking at the floor and feet all around him in the crowded line. He took a deep breath. "I know things are bad, but you think that anarchy group has the answers?"

"It's not anarchy, it's revolution."

"Okay, but replace what we have with what exactly? The Calvinists? You want a militia taking over here?"

Miles pulled a pamphlet from his back pocket. "You've got it all wrong, my friend."

Archer could tell he'd been ready for this moment. Archer snatched the pamphlet from his hand and looked down at the cover. A black upside-down crown on the center of the cover was becoming all too familiar. The symbol covered walls and buildings everywhere these days. He read the title to himself.

THE FEDERAL DECONSTRUCTION MOVEMENT. A Proposal to liberate Americans from tyranny.'

Half the flyer was about the movement itself, and the lower half was an invitation to join the movement.

Miles and Archer were reaching the front of the line. Miles leaned over toward Archer, "Put that away and make sure you read it later. We're almost up."

Chapter Fourteen

29 October

366 Days before the war

Maverick sat on her bed upstairs. It was getting late, just another hour before the household bedtime routine would start—first Leo and Blaze, followed by Mav and Reese, then it used to be Archer, but he didn't have a bedtime anymore since he started working. She was trying to finish her math homework on her laptop to get downstairs and be with everyone else. The window to her room was covered with condensation. She was distracted by the droplets of rain hitting against the glass.

Downstairs, Stan was making hot chocolate in the kitchen for all the kids. This had become the nighttime ritual since it started getting dark earlier. He could hear Leo, Blaze, Reese and Lexi laughing in the living room. As he was stirring the cocoa powder in the pot, he was suddenly startled by the silence. He stopped and listened as the laughter stopped, as if they had vanished.

Stan finally turned around to walk in the living room and was greeted by a shotgun barrel pointed at his head. Stan gasped and dropped the spoon he had been holding. It loudly clanked on the tile floor. Stan saw his reflection in mirrored sunglasses worn by a man several inches shorter than him. He could smell the man's bad breath. He was trembling.

"We don't want to hurt anyone," the man blurted out. "We're just taking some food and we'll be on our way." The man positioned himself behind Stan and walked him into the living room. He walked in to see Lexi holding Blaze and Leo on the couch as she tried to cover their heads. He could hear them whimpering in Lexi's lap. Another man wearing a ski mask was standing over her, holding a pistol near her head. Reese was sitting up against Lexi on the couch, covering her head.

"Sit on the floor, don't be a hero, we'll be gone in a minute." The man with the shotgun said as he tapped Stan's shoulder, prompting him to drop to the floor. Stan sat on the floor and held Reese, covering her with his arms. The man with the shotgun returned to the kitchen.

Mav had closed her laptop. She'd finally finished her homework. She ran down the hall, and as she reached the stairwell, she heard a crash of dishes falling in the kitchen, making her freeze in place. More dishes smashed to the floor. She was confused. She couldn't hear anyone. She slowly walked down the stairs and peered over the covered rail where she could peek down into the living room. She saw her family curled up together with a man standing over them with a gun. Her heart started to pound, and she felt like she was going to faint. She started to pant.

"Hurry up in there!" The man shouted with a raspy voice.

Stan got up on his knees to shift and cover the back of Blaze who was still face first in Lexi's lap. Lexi held a stare at the man, looking into his eyes. "Why are you doing this?" She spoke calmly.

"Shut up!" He shouted, peering into the kitchen. He was getting nervous. He started to pace. "Come on, man, we got to get—"

The man stopped himself and turned toward the staircase. He was met with Maverick holding the .357 pointed at his chest. She was panting, and tears were rolling down her face.

"Oh my God, no Maverick! Put that down!" Stan shouted.

The man pointed his gun at Maverick, and everyone started to yell and shout. Stan started to get up and the man pointed his gun back at Stan and screamed, "Stay down!"

He was waving the gun. "Easy, Frank!" A loud booming voice came from the man holding the shotgun. He entered the living room holding two full trash bags. He dropped the bags to the floor and calmly strolled up toward Maverick. "Everyone, just calm down. We don't need this at all. We'll be out of here and nobody will get hurt." He was a few feet away. Stan was ready to pounce as the man pulled the shotgun from around his back into his hand. "Alright, little girl, you just give me that—"

An explosion from Mav's barrel flashed in the living room. Everyone's ears started to ring. Stan jumped to his feet as both the intruders darted for the door, barreling past Stan. Stan grabbed the gun from Mav—who stood frozen—and started to chase the men out the door. Lexi pushed all the kids upstairs and picked up Maverick who still hadn't moved.

Stan ran to give chase, but the men were gone. A spotted trail of blood showed the men's path out the door. He looked back and forth up and down the street. Were they in a car? By foot?

Lexi frantically tried to dial the police on her cell phone.

Reese took the phone from her hand. She was cool and calm, "I'll call," she said assertively and dialed 9-1-1.

Lexi cupped Maverick's cheeks with her hands, staring into her eyes, "It's okay, sweetheart, you're safe. Everything is going to—"

"I know. I'm okay, Mom," Mav smiled. Tears were still rolling down her cheeks.

Lexi couldn't stop touching all the kids, checking them frantically. She didn't know what to do. Reese was talking on the phone, giving the address and explaining the situation.

Stan heard a car coming up the street. He was still holding the revolver in his hand. Was it them? Were they coming back? Stan ran back toward the house. He could see the headlights in his peripheral vision. He sprinted to get in front of the door. A floodlight from the car beamed onto him.

"Drop the gun, stop right there!" Stan realized it was the police and understood how this all looked. He tossed the revolver out of his hand and threw his arms up in the air, stopping in his tracks. He squeezed his eyes shut, expecting to get ripped apart by bullets. He followed their directions and lay face down on the ground. "My family is inside! We were just robbed!"

"Stay down and don't move!" The voice was slowly getting closer. He could see the dark silhouette of an officer approaching with a handgun pointed at him. "Stan?" The officer gasped. Stan heard the familiar voice. It was Herbert, his therapy client.

Chapter Fifteen

20 October

10 Days before the war

Reese was the first out of bed before the sun came up. That wasn't unusual. She had an extremely busy day planned along with the help of Mav and her mother. She started with gathering up all the blankets and quilts she and her mother were able to create, repair, or salvage and repurpose. Once per week, the school gym, now abandoned from daily school days after shifting to a three-day school week, became a swap meet for all the residents. This started six months ago on the lawn of the local elementary school in the spring with several families meeting and swapping vegetables and clothing. In August, the weekly swap meet moved into the gymnasium. Reese wasn't sure how that worked or who gave permission, but it was better than being outside, especially when it rained.

As the twilight of the morning became more visible, Reese waited patiently for the power to turn on. Since last winter and spring, the power had been on a daily schedule that gradually reduced from being shut off a few hours per day to nearly the entire day. Most recently, power was on for two hours in the morning and evening every day until further notice. As the lights came on, she scrambled eggs and boiled oatmeal for everyone, saving her from having to use the propane stove on the patio.

Reese went out to the garden with several buckets. The peppers were still producing even though they were wilted and ready to die. This was likely the last of them for the season. She was able to fill a bucket of bell peppers and one bucket of banana peppers. Green beans and crowder peas were also doing well, and she was able to fill two buckets of them. Finally, the spaghetti squash. This monstrosity nearly overtook the entire garden with its vines that stretched nearly fifty feet and attempted to choke out all the other plants. Over the last two months, she was able to pull dozens of large spaghetti squash. Now, they were small, like the size of an eggplant.

As Reese brought in the last of the buckets around her assembled pile to take to the swap, Mav sleepily entered the kitchen, wiping her eyes. "Reese, why'd you do all this? I could have helped you."

Reese shrugged her shoulders. "Why do I have to ask? Nobody has to ask me?"

"Reese, come on." Mav was frustrated. She didn't know what to say, and Reese wasn't telling her. "I mean, what do I need to do?" I'll be sure to help out more and take the load off you."

"We're just different now. There's nothing wrong."

Mav couldn't argue her point. Things weren't like they were a year ago when they were in school. Reese was becoming herself. An independent person capable of so much more than she or anyone knew.

Lexi and Stan shuffled into the kitchen as well. "Hey, hey! You girls did all this? Look at you two, up and at 'em." Stan said, smiling the best he could for being so tired.

Mav quickly interjected, "It was all Reese. I'll get the canning jars."

Forest View Elementary School was a short distance, and they walked over carrying all the items they wanted to trade. Leo and Blaze had backpacks full of jars. Many were empty to be reused and many full of green beans, zucchini relish, and apples for trade. Reese had made quite a lot of friends among all the neighbors. She had her notebook that she kept handy to keep track of who was growing what. Reese was exceptionally patient and efficient at canning. Most people didn't have the patience for it. Reese had started collecting fruits and vegetables to can and would complete the task for others as long as they provided the jars and lids. She'd keep one in 5 jars she was able to can as a service fee, then return the empty jars once they were emptied. It worked well for everyone.

The gym was already crowded with residents who brought blankets and tables to set up and trade wares. While people were still able to purchase limited supplies at the stores on their scheduled shopping days, many didn't have money to purchase as much anymore, and produce had long been gone from the official markets. Here, people were able to trade goods and even services as well. Haggling and bartering were a must. Stan left all that to Lexi and Reese. Together, they had made several deals for childcare, tailoring, canning, etc. Mav, Archer and Stan often offered services for manual labor.

They usually stayed for hours. The Neighbors also had a meeting there at the time to pick up the schedule for the roving watch. People brought instruments and played songs and often stayed until the power came back on in the evening.

Chapter Sixteen

1 November

363 days before the war

Lexi had hardly slept over the last three days since the break-in. Nobody in the home was sleeping well. Lexi was wide awake in bed, staring at the alarm clock set to go off in two minutes. She kept playing the night over and over in her mind. She was worried about all the kids but especially Mav. Stan had been sure to keep talking about what happened with all the kids. He would try to answer all their questions. Leo and Blaze were asleep in their bed. They'd been sleeping with them since that night. She slowly rolled over to her feet, careful not to wake anyone and turned the alarm clock off with seconds to spare.

Lexi was tying her robe and heading to the hallway. She stopped at Mav and Reese's door. She couldn't hear any sound. She slowly and quietly opened the door, peering in to see her daughters asleep in their beds. This was the third time she had done this since last night. This time, she quietly walked in and sat on the edge of Mav's bed. She stared at her sleeping face and touched her long brown hair. Mav opened her eyes and jolted. "Mom?" Mav widened her eyes, then rubbed them. "What's wrong?"

Lexi smiled. "Nothing, sweetheart." Mav turned toward the window and checked the clock. "Are we going to school today?" Lexi shook her head, "Not today."

"Why? This will be the third day. I want to go back."

"I know. I just want—" Lexi paused and thought about her words. "It's Friday. You guys can go back Monday, okay?"

Maverick nodded her head and placed it back on the pillow. Her eyes got heavy, and she fell back to sleep. Lexi was worried. Mav didn't seem phased at all and didn't want to talk about what happened. Whenever it got brought up, she would try to change the subject and argue that she was fine. Lexi and Stan were not in agreement about school. He said she needs to go back as soon as possible to get some routine and normalcy. Lexi didn't want to let her out of her sight.

Three nights ago, the family had been interviewed by the police as reports were taken. The .357 revolver was taken into evidence with no likely way to get it back soon that they knew of. The armed assailants were never found, according to the police. The investigation was still "open." Sketches were drawn, but the glasses and masks made them useless. Herbert had told Stan before leaving the home that most likely, nothing else would come of it, unless for some reason the two men turned themselves in. Which also meant he'd likely never get his revolver returned from evidence, especially with short staff and the way crime was increasing so much.

Lexi had made a pot of coffee as she sat at the table listening to the brewing sounds of the old appliance. She lifted her notebook screen and opened a document that she had nearly finished writing. It was addressed to Bob, the quick-tempered neighbor from the HOA meeting that demanded a neighborhood watch. She had written a letter to Bob and several other members requesting to formally create a watch group. After reading several websites about this, she had proposed to make a schedule of rovers at night throughout the neighborhood. She planned to visit Bob first. She was a little concerned about his demeanor, but this was imperative in her mind.

"Yo! Mom!"

Lexi jumped and spilled her coffee on her robe as Archer strolled into the kitchen. "Sorry, Mom," Archer said as he stopped in front of the table. Everyone was still very jumpy since the break-in. He felt insensitive. When Archer had returned from work three nights ago to see the emergency lights and cars outside the house, he was extremely scared that someone was dead. He panicked. He had told his parents he wanted to quit his job to stay home and make sure the house was secure at night. It was a nice gesture, but Stan wouldn't have it. Not for that reason. His mother agreed that he may be able to participate in the neighborhood watch as long as they were at least in pairs. Archer was still going to school while the rest of the kids had stayed home.

"Do you work tonight?" Lexi asked while wiping spilled coffee with a rag.

"Yeah, right after school. I have some seeds on hold for me along with some other stuff. This guy, Calvin, I was telling you about, has been really helpful. He just seems to know everything. I want Evelyn to meet him, I think she'd like him." Archer was looking in the fridge and realized his mother didn't respond. "Mom? You okay?"

"Oh, yeah. Sorry." Lexi started to cry.

Archer went to her and gave her a hug. "It's going to be okay," he said.

***

Four o'clock came slow for Stan. It wasn't just the end of the day. It was his scheduled session with Herbert. Stan was a little anxious to see him. Herbert was the first officer at the scene three nights ago and led the investigation. Stan was so relieved that it had been a friendly face. That helped the situation a lot.

Herbert came into the office as he always had, wearing a ball cap with a law enforcement logo, jeans and a t-shirt. They shook hands like usual, but Stan shook it longer. Stan started to feel big emotions welling up. He wanted to hug him, but instead directed him to his usual seat and sat down.

"How you holding up?" Herbert asked. Stan felt like it was his therapy session today.

"Yeah, we're doing okay. It's been scary and odd."

"You did everything you could. Your family's safe."

Stan nodded his head in feigned agreement. He stopped nodding and started to shake his head. "No, I don't think so, Herbert. I kept my head in the sand. I should have been more cautious. I should've—"

"Everyone is okay," Herbert interjected. "Now you'll do things a little differently."

Stan laughed and smiled, "Thanks, doc." They both chuckled. Stan stared down at the floor, "I had a dream they came back. You know, looking for revenge."

"They aren't coming back."

"Yeah, I know. The likelihood is—"

"No, Stan," Herbert interjected again, leaning forward in his seat. "I'm telling you, they aren't coming back."

Stan stared into Herbert's eyes and paused. "What do you mean?"

Herbert sat back in his seat and looked up at the ceiling with a face like he was trying to select his words carefully. He gave a quizzical look at Stan. "This is all confidential, right?"

"Yes."

"I mean, If I am going to kill myself or kill someone else you have to say something, right?"

"Yes." Stan responded slower and started to feel worried.

"Okay, what if a client maybe did something that might be illegal or unethical or something, but nobody was physically harmed?"

"Well, yes. Confidentiality would stay intact."

Herbert continued to stare into Stan's eyes. "Three hours after your break-in, there was an 'unrelated incident' that happened several miles away. An officer reported a suspicious parked vehicle with two men inside. He immediately called for backup which was delayed, but I headed out there anyway thinking it might be your guys."

Stan was frozen. He continued to stare at Herbert, completely blank of expression.

"When the officer approached the vehicle, one of the men showed a firearm and the officer shot up the inside, killing both men."

"It was them?"

"Well, officially—according to the report, there was no evidence to suggest that. Something like mirrored sunglasses and ski masks were not... in the report. If they were there, they were somehow lost. The officer swore he only hit one of the men. The one in the driver's seat. However, the passenger had been shot through the chest as well. Maybe it was 'a magic bullet.'"

Stan started to scratch his head. He could feel cold sweat, and his heart began to race.

"Herbert, I don't understand. Why—"

"Because your daughter doesn't need any of this, and your family doesn't need these two wacko's kin or whatever looking for revenge. It's better it stays unrelated and that they were killed by a cop. Officially, we don't know what happened to those guys. They got spooked and ran and one was injured."

Stan started to bite his thumbnail. Sweat dripped down his forehead. "Herbert, I don't know what to say or how to feel. I'm a little confused."

"It's just better this way. Nobody loses from this staying unrelated. It's victimless. I wanted to tell you, because I knew you'd be worried, and I don't blame you. Just keep your doors locked and follow the safety precautions I told you about a few nights ago." Herbert leaned back in his seat. "You're a good man, Stan. You saved my life already and helped me reconnect with my family. It's the least I could do."

Stan took a deep, long breath and exhaled with an affirming nod. He mouthed "thank you" and smiled.

Herbert smiled and nodded. "On another note, I've decided to retire. I'm moving to Georgia."

Stan snapped from his trance and replied, "Oh Herbert, that's great news. What made you decide to take that plunge?"

Herbert removed his ball cap, revealing his balding head with fluffy white hair on the sides and back. He rubbed the top of his head, thinking of a thoughtful response. "Well, it's everything I said before, of course. I'm no alarmist, Stan. But we need the military to keep the peace. Police aren't able to do it anymore. There's riots in Charlotte."

Stan nodded, "I read about that."

Herbert continued, "Grocery stores are getting vandalized and looted. Then there's that new group."

"What group?"

"It's this, I don't know, underground group of terrorists or something. They are apparently getting pretty organized. They're called the Deconstructionists or Decons."

"Huh, I've never heard anything about that."

"Yeah, you probably won't. Feds are all looking into it and keeping a tight lid on it. They're really scared of this. They aren't sure if it's an organization or what exactly. So far, the assumption is it must be something organized. Apparently, this group sees themselves as the real Americans and believe that the United States was taken over by corporate interest or something along those lines."

"That's interesting. So, what have you seen?"

Herbert smiled. "Well, I'm not supposed to really talk about it, but I think you and I are a little past that. Still, I'd appreciate you keeping this to yourself."

"Hey, still confidential." Stan flashed a sly grin.

Herbert chuckled, "That's right. That's right. Well, they may be organizing some of the riots and doing some sabotage. Terrorist kind of stuff, I suppose. It's more of a national movement, but they think it's here too. Only thing I've seen is the mark they leave all around. They use orange spray paint and make this M-looking thing, I guess it's an upside-down crown. They usually leave some threatening messages toward 'loyalists of the crown,' which I suppose is anyone who disagrees with them or maybe just means the U.S. Government. We're not completely sure."

Stan was starting to feel the cold sweat again. "What do they want?"

Herbert shrugged his shoulders, "They want to overthrow the government, I suppose."

Chapter Seventeen

21 October

9 days before the war

"Can we please talk about this?" Stan said, breaking the silence at the table. Archer looked up from his papers sprawled on the kitchen table. The sunlight just started to beam through the kitchen window, creating a glow in Archer's messy hair.

"Talk about what?" Archer continued to read and fill out his induction paperwork. Stan stared silently watching his son. The silence caught up to Archer as he finally looked up to meet his father's eyes. Stan sighed and was trying to get the words out, but he couldn't speak.

"Dad, I have to go. There's nothing to talk about."

"Yes, there is. Look, this isn't World War II or even Vietnam."

"It's a draft for national security."

"We don't know that."

"Well, how do you know then? If I don't go, they'll come for me and put all of us at risk. I won't put you guys in that kind of danger."

Stan started to respond but didn't have an answer. He knew Archer had a point. Stan grabbed his coffee cup and stood up from his chair. Archer watched him quizzically.

"Come with me," Stan whispered and walked toward the back door. Archer rolled his eyes and dropped his pencil on the table. He reluctantly stood up. As he watched his father quickly open the back door and exit outside, Archer grabbed his coat draped over the chair and put it on as he walked toward the door. Archer stood next to his father who was looking at the backyard. Raised garden beds covered the entirety of the yard.

"This was us. This was our work. I can't do this without you here. I need your help. There's no school anymore, you're not working at a job, we can hide you here." Stan pleaded.

"I know, Dad."

"We need you here."

"Dad. It's not about hiding. There's a part of me that thinks something bigger than our family has to happen to change what's going on in the world. Maybe I could be part of that change."

"Archer, I was not born yesterday. I've known you your whole life. You have never been someone to join a crusade. You aren't very patriotic. Just admit it and stop playing me for a fool. You're joining because of Evelyn."

Archer ran his fingers through his hair. "I'll admit that's a big part."

"Archer, I'm no military expert, but I think the chances of you being stationed where she is are... astronomical. Do you know how many people are in the Army and how spread out they are?"

Archer reluctantly nodded. "Yeah, but she's fighting and I'm not. How would you feel if Mom was in the army and you weren't?"

Stan nodded. He took a loud, slurping drink from his cup. "I get that. I do. I can see how you'd feel that way. But there's a bigger picture here. What if joining the military is actually adding to the problem?"

Archer turned his head and shot his father a confused look. "The government is the problem? You think the Deconstructionists are the answer? Should I join the Calvinists?"

Stan turned, faced his son, and tossed the remaining coffee into the garden. "Hey, no, I'm not saying that. You know, it's not just one or the other. I'm saying I think the answer is neither. I think there's going to be a war here. This draft is not just for security at some grocery store, I can promise you that. This is not our war. We need to stay together, right here, so we can survive."

Archer shrugged his shoulders. "I don't know what the right choice is." He put his hands in his jacket pockets and withdrew the flyer Miles had given him yesterday.

"What's that?" Stan was curious.

"Nothing, I just had it in my pocket. Miles gave this to me."

"Let me see that," Stan grabbed the flyer and opened it. "Where'd this come from?"

Archer shrugged, "I told you, Miles gave it to me. He's all into the Calvinist movement. He joined the 6th Brigade and even got a tattoo... moron."

Stan unfolded the flyer. "Having something like this on you could get you arrested if the wrong people see it. This is a recruitment flyer for the Calvinists."

"No. I know. I just forgot." Archer was getting frustrated. He turned around toward the door. "I'm going back inside."

Stan watched Archer close the door and stood feeling defeated. He just couldn't seem to convince him and felt so powerless. Stan straightened out the paper. It was a sheet with tiny typeface writing, listing the demands to the federal government and a generic plan for dismantling it. Stan was able to find a magnifying glass in a box in the garage full of old office supplies from his previous job at the County. The flyer read that the Federal Deconstruction Movement was a plan to save America and that the country had been taken over by powerful oligarchs who controlled the bureaucracy and had extinguished all power of the people. The FDM was reportedly made up of many Americans working together to overthrow the bureaucracy and leave the people to govern themselves, as was the original intent by the founders of the Constitution.

'Sovereignty to the states, Sovereignty to the counties, Sovereignty to the people.'

Stan scoured through the writing. He was looking to see what they proposed as a replacement to the system. There was nothing, just John Locke quotes about the right to revolt and the right to overthrow tyranny. There was no suggested replacement of the government in any way. It stated that people have the right to govern themselves based on their own beliefs and ideologies. The movement has the right to ensure that power is never to exceed the state level or it will be subject to dismantling.

In large letters was an invitation to join a local organization that claimed to have all the rights and authority to exist under the deconstruction movement. A phone number was written on the sheet in blue ink with an underlined statement,

'Ask for Calvin.'

Chapter Eighteen

2 November

362 days before the war

The family was up early, as was the usual routine for the last several weeks. The beds were set in long rows, leaving two feet apart to get around. The beds reached from the short concrete patio to the end of the fence in long rows about four feet wide. Stan gave up on turning over the soil and so did everyone else. They ended up covering the rows with wet cardboard, killing the grass beneath. They covered the cardboard with mulch, soil from Screws and Planks which took several weekends and more mulch. They were able to find manure that was being given away from a small farm down the road, out of the housing development. Archer was able to convince Miles to use his truck to haul two loads. Archer made Mav wash out the truck bed with a hose when it was complete. The manure was used to start the compost, and leaves and other carbon were added and mixed. They were ready this weekend to try and plant green beans, Swiss chard, squash and zucchini. They figured they might have been too late with frost, but it was worth a try.

Reese had the most endurance. She could stay outside and work constantly and complained the least. Mav avoided the work the most and

Stan always seemed to have something he had to do. Everyone seemed to follow Reese's lead, who just had a natural talent for making everything work in the garden.

Mav, Reese, Leo and Blaze had stayed out of school the entire week. They were told they would go back on Monday. Lexi was nervous to have them go back. She felt nervous the entire week, any time any of the kids left her sight, even Archer. They worked the entire morning and afternoon in the garden. The work was tiring for everyone. Lexi and Stan were worried it wouldn't pay off, but they also felt it had to.

Lexi was juggling the schedule for the day in her head. She had worked out a meeting for the afternoon at Bob's house to discuss the neighborhood watch. That meeting was immediately followed by another at Phoebe's house, along with several others in the community, to discuss setting up a swap for items and food in the community. She was thinking about possibly cutting the last meeting short to make sure she had time to get everyone ready for dinner with Willow's parents. Stan and Archer agreed to make Rice and chicken. It was the last of the protein they had, which she was hoping to stretch another day beyond. Archer agreed to give some cash toward groceries this week since this dinner was entirely his fault.

***

Stan had arrived for the second LEPC meeting. He was wearing sweatpants and a T-shirt, covered with red clay and soil. He nearly forgot about the meeting and didn't have time to change.

"Thanks for dressing up, Stan," Brenda said with sarcasm. Stan shrugged his shoulders and gave a half-hearted apology. He sat down just as the meeting was going to start. Stan didn't have time to explain to

Brenda or anyone else what had happened over the week with the break in at his house. He figured he would tell her after.

Brenda stood up in front of the whiteboard as she did at the first meeting with a marker in hand. She started to write down a list of communication bulletin numbers on the dry-erase wall. She explained that there were official communications regarding the distribution of goods and scheduled days and times for residents to shop based on their zip code. Brenda also reported that there was a bulletin release for proposed rolling blackouts to conserve energy due to the shortage of fuel, natural gas, etc. This news was not a complete shock to everyone as the internet and news outlets had been buzzing about other states that had already implemented these measures. The final bulletin was the announcement of a curfew within certain parts of the counties to address recent protests and riots. After Brenda wrote these words on the board, the sound of clicking tongues and sighs filled the room with disappointment.

Brenda capped the marker in her usual fashion and said, "The first one is our priority. The other two are soon to come." She directed everyone to write questions on paper in front of them rather than ask out loud until the discussion was complete. All grocery stores in the county would be managed and taken over as distribution sites. She laid out a vague plan that allowed several days available to everyone. An ID was required and would be provided if they had none. The subcommittee discussed first how it was proposed to be rolled out, then the questions came.

Stan raised his hand first. "Brenda, this doesn't sound like a plan that's going to work well in reality. I mean, I have seven in my family, you have two. Other people are single. I don't think having equal time by household will work." Brenda nodded and seemed to have already thought of this question.

"That's why everyone can go five days per week. There's actually more time you can be at the store than not."

Stan shrugged, "Yeah for now. I have a feeling this setup with the number of windows will get less and less over time."

"Look how it is now." Brenda shot back, seemingly defensive. "We've had three stores completely overrun in the last month. Too many people go at the same time and it turns into chaos."

Stan didn't want to get into a big argument but couldn't help himself. "I get that, but what happens if you need something right now, like medicine?"

"Then go to the pharmacy or a smaller general store. This is only for the grocery stores listed." Brenda answered and seemed determined to move on.

Stan ran his fingers through his hair. Another member asked about transportation and what would happen to those who don't have cars. Brenda just answered that they would get there the same way they have been before this was implemented. Limits would also be the same everywhere and not created store to store. Inventory would also be the same in all locations. The plan was set to go into effect in one month from that day.

***

Lexi arrived at Bob's door in the late morning as planned and rang the doorbell. She left Archer, Mav and Reese to watch Leo and Blaze. Even though she was two blocks away, she was worried about them and fought off the intrusive thoughts of another break-in. Just as the ruminating memory of Mav pulling the trigger played out in her mind, she startled back to the present moment at the click of the deadbolt. Bob's wife Wendy answered the door with a smile and a friendly greeting.

In the living room, she was greeted by Bob and several others from the neighborhood she didn't recognize. After they made their introductions, Bob asked Lexi how the family is holding up after the break-in. The word traveled through the neighborhood rather quickly.

Lexi smiled, "We're hanging in there. That was the scariest thing I ever encountered in my life and it's still always on my mind."

Bob was supportive but seemed to use her words as a jumping point. "I was lucky. The break in here, we didn't get threatened like that. We can't count on the police, and we need to protect each other." Everyone nodded in agreement. Bob had a poster he drew of a map of the Forest View housing development and placed it on the coffee table in front of him. His finger trembled as he pointed to the two roads leading into and out of the development. "From everything I've heard from anyone whose house has been broken into, all the bad guys showed up and left in cars. Doesn't sound like they're ever on foot. We want to watch these two roads. There's no other way in or out for cars. Depending on how many volunteers we have, we'd at best want two people watching the roads and two rovers."

"Rovers?" Lexi asked. She knew what a rover was but wanted to hear more.

"Yep, a pair together that randomly walks the streets. Everyone communicates using a radio, and we do regular check-ins. Chuck here has agreed to try to make a schedule. He was a yeoman in the Navy, and I think he's an expert on this kind of stuff. What do you say, Chuck? What would a week look like for a volunteer?"

Chuck, whom Lexi had never met or even seen before, opened his laptop and studied the screen. "If we covered from say 8:00 p.m. to 6:00 a.m., seven days per week, that would be ten hours per night, and let's say we break that into two five-hour shifts. We'd need 56 volunteers for each to have one five-hour shift per week. How many volunteers do we have so far?"

Lexi pulled her phone out and went to her notes as she was selected to recruit volunteers. "Looks like twenty-seven so far," she answered with a frown.

"Remember, that's in a perfect world. Some are willing to take more shifts, but I recommend no more than two per week. We can also rotate the times.

"Lexi, when you can, would you ask if anyone would be willing to take two shifts?"

Lexi agreed and typed out a text to the group. As she was typing, she asked, "What will someone on the shift be doing?"

Bob cleared his throat. "Well, the two watching the roads will just be doing that and reporting cars on the radio that come in. The rovers will be watching and listening for anything suspicious."

"And what do they do if there's something suspicious?"

"That's what we need to talk about."

"Are we going to be armed?"

"I'd definitely recommend it," Bob replied assertively.

Lexi thought for a moment, "Aren't you a little worried about that?"

Bob looked in her eyes, "I'd be more worried if we weren't armed."

***

After his meeting concluded, Stan walked across the street to the Sheriff's substation. He requested a gun release application to formally request getting his .357 back that was taken as evidence from the previous night. Herbert had told him exactly which form to request and what to say in the request. He was surprised to find out it was ready to be released but might be confiscated again at the request of law enforcement.

After sitting in the lobby for nearly an hour, Stan's Ruger GP100 was given back to him, sealed in a plastic bag. He felt a chill seeing it again, especially noticing the powder marks on the cylinder and frame from Mav pulling the trigger.

As Stan got back to his car, he noticed orange graffiti crudely sprayed on the wall of an abandoned store across the street. He walked up to the concrete wall with old, peeling brown paint to inspect it; an orange three-point, upside-down crown with writing that said

'REVOLT IS THE RIGHT OF THE PEOPLE.'

***

Lexi was checking her watch and jogging back home. The meeting at Bob's house to discuss the neighborhood watch went longer than expected. She had planned to run by the house to take Reese with her to the next meeting. Reese was standing outside the door on the porch, holding a notebook.

"What are you doing out here?" Lexi snapped.

Reese shrugged her shoulders, bewildered, "I'm just standing here, what's wrong?"

Lexi caught her breath and thought for a second before responding. She realized she was being overly anxious again, "Nothing, you ready?"

Phoebe's husband was outside in the front yard of their house two blocks away. He had started turning over the front lawn using a gas-powered tiller. This was happening more in the neighborhood every day. The HOA and its usual authority were seemingly nonexistent at this point, especially since the last meeting.

The living room was full of neighbors, some Lexi had seen and others she had not. As soon as she saw the full crowd with standing room only, she thought maybe bringing Reese was not a great idea. She looked over, expecting the deer-in-the-headlights look and puffy red cheeks. Surprisingly, she didn't. Reese took her notebook out and started to scribble. It took some time to get going, but eventually Phoebe started the meeting and addressed everyone in the room. There was some disagreement on how to proceed. Some had suggested they just have a swap meet in an open area, others were suggesting more structure and using the internet for people to post what they have for sale or trade.

The discussion was back and forth, and several were starting to talk out of turn. Suddenly, Reese interjected, "Why don't we do both? We use an app so everyone can post their requests and what they have. Everyone can look at it and know what they are after, so the swap meet can go quicker or they can just make contact on their own." Lexi was stunned, she hadn't seen Reese this assertive since 5th grade.

"And who's going to manage all that, especially online?" Someone from the living room interjected.

"I can, it's not that hard," Reese replied with genuine confidence about her skills. "I'll make one list for fruits, vegetables, and whatever other food, another for tools, another for supplies and stuff."

Phoebe smiled and in perhaps a patronizing tone replied, "I like your determination. But that may take a lot of time and energy, Renee."

Reese had a serious look on her face. "It's Reese, and I can do this. It'll be easy."

Phoebe smiled, "Well, thank you. Let's see how that goes. I think that would be helpful—"

"Speaking of helpful," Reese interrupted, "you have a tiller. I haven't seen anyone else with one. Tilling this clay with a pickaxe is impossible for most of us. My dad and my brother are pretty strong, and they even gave up on it. You could be very helpful sharing that tiller."

Everyone in the living room started to mumble and nod their heads. Phoebe appeared uncomfortable. "Well, I'm not sure. That's more of my husband's thing. I don't know what he wants to do with it."

"I'm not saying you loan it out for free. Just think about what it is you need. I know you guys are asking for babysitting a lot. So, we can work out trades that are more than just for food and supplies but also for things we can do for each other."

"Like trading services," Lexi interjected, "that's a great idea."

Reese thought for a second. "That tiller needs gas. If someone wants to use the tiller, you show them how to use it right and loan it out for a set number of hours. They need to have their own gas and use it themselves. In exchange, have them babysit for a couple of days."

The residents seemed to light up with ideas and were all talking at the same time. Phoebe nodded, "That's a really good idea, Reese. Okay, everyone, please"

The living room slowly became quiet. "Why don't we all write down not only what supplies we need and have to trade but also, like Reese said, services we can provide and services we are in need of?"

Lexi couldn't help but smile.

***

Stan and Archer were arguing about the way to properly cover chicken in the oven, as well as the amount of seasoning to use. Evelyn was trying to defuse the nonsensical argument and explain that either way would work. Besides the Spanish rice Stan made, they also had enough potatoes to spare as another side dish. Evelyn had brought over a casserole dish of baked mac and cheese which helped as well. A simple and considerably bland meal in the past, but today it was extremely hardy and difficult to come by.

Lexi and Reese arrived at home with enough time to get Leo and Blaze dressed and ready as well. Mav, surprisingly, was still in the backyard finishing a mulch covering on the last bed.

Willow and her parents arrived at the house a few minutes early. They brought a carton of eggs laid by their chickens, a jar of hard apple cider and squash casserole with ingredients mostly from their garden. While stressful, Lexi and Stan were relieved to meet Willow's parents, Brett and Jenny Filmore. It was nice to socialize with adults again in just a friendly capacity and not have to focus on work or just plain survival.

Archer was being surprisingly well-mannered and made introductions. Evelyn and Lexi were both silently impressed.

After dinner, the girls ran upstairs to see Mav and Reese's room. Leo and Blaze continued their usual loud ruckus in the living room with their toys strewn about. Archer and Evelyn stayed at the table with Archer's parents and the Filmore's.

Brett poured several small glasses of hard cider. He looked at the empty fifth and sixth glass and held the jar above it making eye contact first with Archer who nodded with a big grin, then Stan.

Stan laughed at Archer's grin and said, "yeah, sure." Stan started to think about how much Archer had grown in such a short time and how responsible he'd become. As for Evelyn, well, he wasn't her dad.

"I just wanted to share with you guys some of the fruit of our labor, I guess you could say. Everything we brought here is from our home. Archer here told us that you guys are trying to learn to homestead. I was right where you all were not too long ago."

Stan held up his glass and smiled, "Well, we really appreciate you coming over and bringing all this. Cheers!" Everyone repeated and took a drink of the cider.

Brett looked out the sliding glass door at the backyard and stood up, "can we take a look?"

They all walked single file out into the backyard, "It's such a mess," Lexi expressed with aspiration.

"Oh yeah, but that's a good thing," Jenny answered with a smile. Both Brett and Jenny were extremely positive and made them feel like the earth is more forgiving and flexible than they thought. The key, they said, was to just keep it up and be patient. Brett had told them a way to rotate the crops and showed them which beds might work best to start. He encouraged growing legumes and other plants that fix nitrogen so others like peppers can grow better in the bed after the beans are gone. He also mentioned wild plants that can be used like dandelions, wild onions, and even pokeberry leaves before they grew and turn red—definitely not the berries, which are poisonous.

They had gone back into the house as the last of the daylight faded and continued to talk. Both Brett and Jenny had been in the army, which is where they met. They both completed several tours in Iraq and Afghanistan between them. This got Evelyn very excited as she explained her career goals, which she always took every opportunity to do. The conversation veered toward the current state of things. It was difficult not to.

Lexi lamented, "I'm just so scared. This was always a hobby I wished I could get myself to do. Now we need it. It's a necessity and not a hobby."

Brett nodded, "I definitely agree. The food in the stores is getting harder to obtain, and I'm afraid one day we won't be able to even go to a grocery store anymore, not unless you're rich."

Stan was about to say something regarding the LEPC meeting, but remembered he needed to keep that to himself. Lexi looked at Archer, remembering how she didn't like talking about this with the kids around. She realized sitting at this table, he wasn't a kid anymore.

She started to rub her hands together, "I used to think things would improve, that they have to."

Brett nodded, "I think they will."

Stan was surprised and curious, "Do you?"

Brett continued to nod and seemed to be choosing his words carefully, "I think it will be very different. And I think it will get worse first, but I think it will get better."

Lexi was now intrigued and replied, "I'd love to hear some good news for a change."

Brett exchanged a look with Jenny. "Have you heard of the Federal Deconstruction Movement?" Lexi and Archer shook their heads, but Stan didn't.

Stan felt his pulse spike. "I have."

"I have, too," Evelyn added.

"What've you heard?" Brett asked, giving an intrigued look.

Stan looked at Evelyn as she gave a wave for him to talk first. He took a deep breath. He regretted saying he had heard of it at that moment. He shrugged his shoulders, "Not very much. I heard it's like a terrorist organization. They leave graffiti. I don't know. Not much." He looked over at Evelyn, hoping she'd step in.

Evelyn set her cup of Cider on the table. "It's a slogan. You know, like a hashtag of sorts. Like Eat the Rich or MeToo. It's an anti-American slogan for overthrowing the government and the constitution."

Brett gave a slight chuckle and smile, "Well, that doesn't surprise me at all."

Archer broke the silence, "I'm sorry, what is the deconstruction movement?"

Jenny giggled at Archer's innocent question. "Like Evelyn said, it's not an organization, it's a belief. Well, some of us believe it's the truth, to be honest."

"And that truth is?" Lexi gripped her own hands and was nervous about what was coming next.

"That we have a constitutional right and duty to overthrow tyranny. We're in a system that has total control and power, not just of the country, but the world. Our leaders are Oligarchs who are using our labor and resources to fuel wars in foreign countries so that they alone can profit. What we have now is the result of it. We get nothing, and the few at the top get everything. It's our responsibility to resist and overthrow that. To give power back to the people. We want local government with self-sufficiency. We're all dependent on this food controlled by the elite, that's barely fit to eat. That part is going to get worse, but it will change one way or the other."

Evelyn shook her head. "But we've had civil war before. That won't make life better. We need unity right now."

Brett nodded his head in agreement, "Well said. I know what you're saying, and my whole life up to recently, I agreed with that notion. I think we need to face the reality that our country has already been overrun by corrupt, powerful oligarchs, and we are trying to get our country back so we can have unity the way it was supposed to be."

Stan started to get a bad feeling and was tempted to just let it go. "That sounds great, but even taking the country back would mean someone else comes into power, so what is it replaced with? Usually, it's just one tyrant for another." The words left his mouth before he could think. He didn't want to argue with his guests and was becoming fond of them.

Jenny nodded her head. "I think you're right, and it's a very valid point. I don't think any revolution is going to be easy. But how much more do we take? We are talking about learning to be self-sufficient so we can care for ourselves and our community. I do think it's going to get worse and they're going to try to prevent that."

"How?"

"If Martial law gets declared, that will be the flashpoint."

"Wait, what do you mean?"

Brett put his hand on Jenny's to calm her down. "Look, what Jenny's saying is, if it ever gets to where the federal government tries to prevent us from growing our own food or interfere with local commerce, there will be a response to defend ourselves."

Stan leaned back in his chair. Archer finally broke the silence again, "Okay, once again, my apologies, but I feel like we're talking about something without really talking about it and I'm getting lost here."

Lexi interrupted, "I don't understand. I watch the news, sometimes borderline obsessively and I have never seen anything about this. If there was some army or something waiting to start a war, I think we'd hear about this."

Brett nodded, "True. There is no massive underground army. There is no secret organization. The deconstruction movement is a rallying cry, like Evelyn said. It's the movement that gives us the authority to resist, overthrow and govern ourselves. There's local movements of all shapes and sizes popping up all over the U.S. that are empowered by the movement. The graffiti that Stan is referring to is our symbol. We call it the distressed crown. It's an upside-down, three-point crown. The three points symbolize words we are all familiar with—life, liberty and happiness."

Stan put his palm to his forehead and looked up to the ceiling, "Alright, not a secret or central organization. I buy that. But is there a local one?

Brett paused. He was reluctant to answer. "Yes. Yes, there is."

Stan let out a sigh. "Oh man. Can you elaborate?"

"We're not a secret. We are locally organized and all committed to defending the Constitution where we reside."

"Like a militia?" Evelyn asked as if she knew the answer, "Which is illegal, by the way."

"Well, sure. That's the closest thing to it. We are here to protect the rights of the citizens and cover three counties, including this one. Jenny and I are part of the Sixth Brigade, Foxtrot Company. We're all local and live where we serve. The deconstruction movement is what grants us the authority to revolt. Our brigade is under the command of Commander Calvin Eastridge. They call us the Calvinists."

"Isn't that the name of a religious reformation or something?" Evelyn sneered suspiciously.

Brett seemingly forced a laugh, "Yeah, it was actually a dig. You know, a derogatory name. We liked it, so we owned it."

Evelyn was getting visibly upset and frustrated at Brett's audacity. She finished off the cider in her glass and set it on the table. She looked at Stan and Lexi. "I can't even think of what this is going to look like if there's any kind of conflict with the federal government." She was trying to keep her composure and direct the conversation away, but she couldn't. She snapped her head at Brett and Jenny, "I mean, think about it. Drones, guided missiles, air strikes, nuclear weapons. How could this end without everyone, and mostly innocent civilians, getting slaughtered?"

Brett's politeness was starting to fade as well. You could see it on his face. "Sure, they got all that. And you better hear this, if they drop bombs on any civilians, I can promise you every man, woman, and child would be in Washington D.C, and that administration will hang—but, to your point, you need to think about where you are. Didn't you grow up here? The Revolutionary War was right here. Battle of King's Mountain, Battle of Cowpens. That was all right here. This is the Hornets' Nest, and that was the name given by the British. I know the times are different and the technology is different, but I promise you that spirit did not go away."

Brett started to notice he was sounding angry and stopped himself. Everyone sat silent.

Archer perked his head up, "Wait a minute, Calvin Eastridge. I know that guy."

***

Mav and Reese brought Willow into their bedroom. "Do you guys ever get cramped in here?" Both girls nodded their heads in unison.

"You know, my house is only like a half mile if you cross the river, we could literally walk to each other's homes."

Mav tilted her head, thinking about that. "The closest bridge is way out that way," she pointed toward the interstate.

"Haven't you been on the trail? There's a river island not far from here. You can easily cross it. I'll show you next time."

Reese opened her laptop and started typing away. She had several stacks of papers she had received from Phoebe's house with requests and what people had available. Reese started looking for an app that could be used to make it simple.

Willow started to rummage through Reese's stacks of paper. "What's all this?"

"I'm trying to organize a way for everyone around here to trade things."

"A barter system. Yeah, my parents go to swap meets. You could set up something like that around here."

"Everyone just needs so much stuff, and it's hard to stay organized."

"When I've gone, people set up their own tables with stuff they have. Then they all have a little sign of the top five to ten things they need. Then they just talk about it and make trades."

Reese looked up at Willow, "Yeah. That makes sense. That way everyone can say what they want themselves and not just have one person like me try to figure it out."

"You can use that stuff and make a bulletin board. Make a 'wanted' side and 'offer' side. You can post that stuff so people can be ready. It'll make it easier."

Reese nodded and smiled. "Yeah! Awesome idea." Willow nodded, "I know."

Willow plopped down next to Maverick sitting on her bed. "Okay. I want to hear all about it. This is the craziest thing I ever heard. Start from the beginning and tell me what happened."

Mav's face soured. "I don't know, I don't like to think about it. I don't know what I was thinking. I was just scared. I remembered where my dad showed me the gun was. I just grabbed it, thinking I didn't want them to take it. I heard Leo and Blaze crying, and I got angry and wanted to protect them. Something like that, I really don't know. It's kind of a blur."

Reese was still typing and staring at the screen, "I'll tell you what happened. She nearly got everyone killed. At least herself anyway. Everyone is still upset about it, but not Maverick. Nope, she's just acting like nothing ever happened."

"Reese! Just stop." Maverick pleaded. She lay down on her bed and hugged her pillow. Willow looked back and forth between them awkwardly. Oddly, she couldn't think of anything to say.

Chapter Nineteen

22 October

8 days before the war

An emergency session was being held in the morning for the LEPC. Stan regretted accepting the board position several weeks ago and preferred the lax rules and expectations of the ad hoc subcommittee which he did remain part of with Brenda who continued to chair. Stan was responsible for directly reporting the findings and recommendations of the subcommittee to the regional LEPC in Charlotte.

He received a text about the meeting that was actually sent the night before but had just shown up on his phone. Cell service for the past six months was spotty at best. SMS text was often delayed, sometimes for several hours. The text said to report to the local office rather than Charlotte.

Stan arrived at the county building before 8:00 a.m. The parking lot and building were empty. He was early, but not that early. He figured this was a mistake or perhaps the meeting was on a previous day, and he missed it. Stan noticed three cars with government plates in the lot by the front door, so he decided to check. He picked up the .357 he left on the passenger seat and opened the cylinder to check it. He thought for a moment, then put the revolver into the glovebox.

He entered the building through the front door and took a step inside. As he closed the door, the silence was deafening, and not a soul was in view. He could hear his breathing. Stan started to feel uneasy. He turned back to exit the door.

"Ah, Mr. Jenkins," came a familiar voice echoing through the lobby. *"Mr. Jenkins, please, thank you for coming."* Stan turned around to notice Mr. Fredrickson from last week's meeting quickly walking toward him with a big smile. Behind him, standing in the doorway of a meeting room, stood Agent Sorenson. No smile to be seen. *"I was afraid you may not have received my message with the way cell service is."*

"The message said there was an emergency session."

"Oh, indeed, Mr. Jenkins. Please, right this way." Mr. Fredrickson held his arm out, pointing back toward Agent Sorenson. Now Stan felt very uneasy. He felt himself walking toward Mr. Fredrickson, but it felt like his mind and consciousness stayed behind. *"You remember my counterpart, Agent Sorenson?"* Agent Sorenson didn't flinch and continued to stare like a stone statue.

"Yeah. Yeah I remember," Stan responded with a tremble in his voice. The walk toward the office felt like it was miles away. He was internally talking to himself, *'I didn't do anything! What do they want?'*

Stan was led into a small conference room and asked to sit at a small round table with three chairs. Mr. Fredrickson and Agent Sorenson followed and sat down. Agent Sorenson still hadn't spoken a word or made a single facial expression. Mr. Fredrickson, likely in his late 50s, smiled broadly. He tipped his glasses up to his nose as he opened a folder on the table. *"Hmm, Mr. Jenkins, yes. Here we are."* Mr. Fredrickson studied a sheet of paper that he held close to his face and lifted his glasses to read. Stan looked at Agent Sorenson and smiled with a brief nod. He didn't reciprocate and just continued to stare uncomfortably. Stan had a lot of questions and remembered that Brenda had told him they were here to question everyone. He tried to keep his lips tight and wait to see what they had to say.

Mr. Fredrickson set the paper down and placed his glasses back on his nose. He smiled and paused. *"Mr. Jenkins, thank you for making the time to meet with us. We are taking this opportunity to discuss some questions with the members of your subcommittee. We understand that you are a select few who have contact on the ground, so to speak, and we'd like to ask about some particular observations."*

Stan shifted in his chair. "Okay."

"So, what is your role in the community?"

"How do you mean?"

"I just mean, I'm curious what qualified you for this position. According to the guidelines, it contains members who are 'stakeholders in the community.'"

"Well, I'm not quite sure. I was asked personally by Brenda Long to join."

Mr. Fredrickson nodded, "I see."

The silence was uncomfortable. Stan felt compelled to say something more. "I guess because I'd worked with her in the past. I've been a therapist in community mental health for many years. Uhm, I don't know, I'm the clinical director of an agency whose main referral source is the county."

Mr. Fredrickson smiled, showing that he appreciated his response and cooperation. "That's excellent, Mr. I'm sorry, is it Doctor Jenkins?"

"No. Just mister."

"My apologies. Mr. Jenkins. It sounds like you've been in contact with many members of the community in many different capacities. I'd like to ask you if you've ever heard of the Federal Deconstruction Movement."

"Of course I have, who hasn't?"

Mr. Fredrickson nodded in agreement, "Yes, yes, of course you have. I mean, have you heard of any activity in the community?"

"There're demonstrations all the time. Lots of banners. I see the graffiti. It's all over, it's true. It seems to have a lot of support. The protests and picketing are everywhere, all the time. Even outside this building. The media, when we can see it, talks about it constantly."

Mr. Fredrickson frowned. He gave a thoughtful look and nodded. "Yes, true." He shuffled more papers from the folder. He withdrew a photograph. "Have you ever met this man? Calvin Eastridge?"

Stan felt his blood pressure rise. He started to sweat. "Yeah. Hard not to know that face around here. Yeah, I've seen him. He's got a lot of support."

"Have you met him personally?"

Stan was stumped. He didn't know what to say. He'd met Calvin Eastridge before, and his son had as well. He didn't want to say that. Stan noticed his words coming out without a formed thought. "I mean, we're not friends or anything. I've seen him in the community. I think he used to go to a local hardware store a lot. He seems to be all over."

"Awe, yes, you're referring to Screws and Planks located on Ferrington Ave. Where your son, Archer Jenkins, was employed, yes?" That was it. Stan snapped. The mention of his son made him see red and feel he was being toyed with.

"Alright, you listen to me, Mr. Fredrickson. I still don't know why you're here or who you even work for. I don't know where you're going with all this, but you need to understand something loud and clear. Me and my family have nothing to do with your nonsense. We just want to be left alone and survive, which is pretty hard to do these days if you haven't noticed. My family isn't part of some crusade, and we don't have a part in any of this government nonsense. So, you leave us alone and leave us out of this. Do you understand me?" Stan found himself on his feet standing over Mr. Fredrickson with his finger pointed at his nose.

"Yes, of course, Mr. Jenkins. My apologies." Mr. Fredrickson flashed his usual smile.

Stan huffed and walked out of the conference room so he wouldn't say anything else. He felt a lump in his throat and was taking heaving breaths, walking through the lobby to the front door.

***

Mav finished her chores around 8:30 a.m. and was in a rush to get out to the South Fork by 9:00 a.m. She didn't have time to change her clothes. She grabbed her compound bow and ran out of the door without saying a word. Forgiveness over permission, she thought. Besides, she was hoping to come home with a rabbit or two to make up for her absence.

127

Mav jogged out to the river trail. And ran parallel to the riverbank about a half mile to the crossing spot on the South Fork. The crossing spot was made up of a wooded river island in the center of the South Fork with a rocky bank on the west side of the river that was relatively easy to traverse without getting wet. The East side had a large log that had toppled years before connecting the bank to the island.

She jumped across several large stones that made a natural path in a shallow area of the river. As she reached the river island, she paused and crouched over to catch her breath.

"There you are!" came a voice from the dense trees. Maverick nodded and held up a finger as she was still trying to catch her breath. Willow emerged from the trees and brush, walking toward Maverick with a big smile. Her bow was slung behind her back. "It's about time. I was about to go on my own."

Mav arched her back to stretch as she started to catch her breath. "I had potatoes to pull, and we're getting ready for the frost. Give me a break."

Willow laughed as she walked up next to her. "You know I'd never leave you behind. We do need to talk about these clothes, though. You're gonna stand out and scare everything away."

"I know, Reese's got me on her list. She's gonna make me some pants and other stuff. How's it been out here?"

"I've seen two Calvinist patrols. No surprise, though, my dad told me to watch for them. They're doing some training exercises too, so maybe your red shirt isn't such a bad idea after all."

They crossed over the log to the east bank and started north on the trail. Willow and Mav had several routes they had planned out over the summer to find rabbits, squirrels and occasional turkeys. They'd rotate traps in each section and had made a schedule to check them. A few times, they'd spotted rabbits in the open and traded off taking shots at them. Willow seemed to never miss. Mav was improving, but so far only bagged two rabbits. Here in the lower foothills of the Appalachians, there weren't many black bears or bobcats to worry about, but they could be spotted from time to time.

"We've got about a half mile or so," Willow said as she hopped over a large, downed branch covering the trail. "When's your brother supposed to leave?"

Maverick tugged on her hoodie sleeve to adjust her glove that kept slipping down, "In just about a week."

"Is he gonna go?"

"I think so. He says he is. He doesn't want us to have any trouble, and he's scared they'll come looking for him. I don't know what's gonna happen. I don't like to think about it."

Willow suddenly stopped and turned around toward Mav. Mav nearly bumped into her before coming to a halt. "What's wrong?"

Willow's eyes moved all around as she stayed frozen. "Do you hear that?"

In the distance, a buzzing like a swarm of hornets started to get louder. The humming and buzzing had a high pitch and sounded eerie.

"Drones. Let's go see!" Willow cut across the brush to the river parallel to the trail and walked onto the sandy bank. Several large drones were flying over the river heading south.

Maverick finally followed, stepping onto the sandy bank next to Willow. "Whose do you think they are?"

Willow shrugged. "My dad says they have some drones for surveillance, but I can't tell." Large surveillance drones had started being spotted more frequently over the last month. A few were even spotted over the Forest View neighborhood.

Chapter Twenty

6 November

358 days before the war

Mav shot up from her pillow with a scream. She was panicking and sweating profusely. She looked around the room and stared at Reese who was still asleep in her bed. "You're here. You're here," she whispered to herself. Mav was still panting and trying to slow her breathing down. She placed her hands on her chest. She looked at her phone to check the time and date, still unsure if this was a dream or reality.

Lexi opened the door, which made Mav startle. "What's wrong?"

Mav shook her head, "Nothing. I'm fine."

"I heard you scream."

"I just had a bad dream."

Lexi came in and sat on the bed next to her. She placed her hand on her cheek, "Oh, you're sweaty. Are you sure—"

"Mom, I'm fine. It was just a dream."

"Was it about the break-in?" Mav didn't answer. "Sweetheart, it's okay to talk to me about it."

Mav started to feel annoyed. "Yes, okay. Yes, I had a dream about what happened. About them coming back. About shooting you guys by accident. All of us getting shot. I've had lots of bad dreams."

Lexi pulled Mav's head to her chest and hugged her tightly. She kissed her on the top of the head. "Come on, let's get up and get some coffee."

"I hate coffee."

"Okay, let's get up and you can watch me drink coffee."

***

After dropping off Blaze and arranging childcare for Leo, Lexi drove to Bob's house for the neighborhood watch meeting. They now had 33 volunteers. Bob's garage door was open when Lexi parked the minivan along the curb. Bob and Chuck both waved as they noticed her walking up the driveway. There were two other neighbors there she'd seen before walking dogs every day. They were in their early 20's.

"Good morning!" Bob said with a big grin. His face had scruffy whiskers, and he wore a very fitted polo shirt from a security company he used to work for. His shirt was tucked in tightly to his cargo shorts. "Thanks so much for coming. Lexi, I'd like you to meet Rand and Steve." Lexi gave a smile and a wave. She recognized their names as two of the six new volunteers. Bob leaned over the large plywood table he had set up in his garage. "I think Rand and Steve will be able to help us with the shortfall we have in personnel. They are both big drone enthusiasts, and I had reached out to see if they could help. They're willing to use some of their gadgets and show some of us how to use them." Rand and Steve both nodded and grinned.

Lexi shot an affirming smile and nod toward them both. "Wow, that's great. I don't know much at all about drones or anything, but if it can help, that sounds wonderful."

"I think the first thing to do is look at planning and prevention. Rand and Steve can use the drones to get a detailed picture of Forest View. We can spot points where there may be vulnerabilities—Trees, bushes, obstacles, you know, places people can hide or park out of sight. Street light blind spots and things like that. Also, we could take a look at people's homes, the exteriors, and let the homeowners know what they could change to make it less vulnerable to break-ins."

Lexi nodded, "I think that sounds like a good idea. Should we tell all the residents what we're doing?"

"Oh, definitely," Bob responded. "And, if anyone don't want our help, that's their business and right. But for everyone else, we could just provide some basics on home security that they can use. For deterrence, you know."

Chuck cleared his throat and interjected, "Another idea, and I'm not sure if this is stepping on toes, but I think it would be helpful to have a list of tag numbers of the cars that belong to the residents. If we see a car that doesn't match, that might help us to identify suspicious vehicles."

Bob gave a slight twinge in his face like he just bit into a sour pickle. The protection of civil liberty was extremely important to him. "I get that, I do. I just feel uncomfortable collecting personal information like that. Your car is your business."

"Maybe we just ask everyone. If they give the information, then great. If not, that's okay too. I think a partial list is more helpful than no list at all," Lexi responded. "Bob, I have a feeling everyone is more willing to cooperate than you think. People are feeling extremely unsafe. Let's give them a chance to tell us what they want. We'll be respectful to anyone who doesn't want to participate."

Chuck affirmed with a hearty nod and grunt. Bob appeared to be considering the idea for a moment and nodded in agreement. Bob then continued. "Well, with that settled, I'd like to talk about some brief training for the volunteers, like basic observation skills, what and when to report, what to do if they find a threat or suspicious activity. I think we can do both tasks at the same time. We can start training and collect info about the neighborhood at the same time. Then we can get started on a schedule. We'll just call it *The Neighbors* until we can think of a better name."

***

Mav and Reese were dropped off at the front of the school by Archer as usual. They walked up the curb facing the front of the middle school's central building. Children were funneling in through the front doors up the steps.

"You doing okay?" Reese asked sympathetically.

Maverick chuckled, "That's usually what I'm asking you." Reese stopped. Mav noticed and turned to face her. "What's wrong?"

Reese's eyes started to well up. "I'm sorry about what I said. That you put us in danger and all that. I don't know why, but I'm just angry about the whole thing. I thought I'd be terrified, but I'm just mad. I don't even know who I'm angry at."

Mav put her arm around her sister to move her along into the building, "I know, I don't know how I feel either. I just want to forget about it."

The halls had fewer students, seemingly every week. Absences had become extremely common in the school system. Many of the kids would show up late for lunch and leave afterward.

Through the hallway, they split off to head to their classes. As Mav turned toward the east wing, she spotted Willow, who was waiting outside the door of her home room class. She noticed Mav and started to head toward her.

"I feel the need!" Willow was nearly shouting and held up her hand for a high five, "The need for speed!" Maverick shook her head smiling and walked past her like she wasn't there. The Top Gun references were getting old. "Hey! Don't leave me hangin', Mav!"

***

It was finally time for Archery class. Maverick had been wanting this all day. The students were now allowed to bring their own bows from home as long as they were secured at the school and kept locked up in the gym and passed a safety check. Willow was extremely giddy all day, and Mav couldn't seem to understand why.

"What's going on with you today?" She finally asked as they walked out to the range.

"You'll see!" Willow laughed and started to hop. They entered the line to retrieve their bows and sign them out. Willow finally broke down as they got close to the front of the line.

"Okay, okay, okay. I got you an early birthday present."

"My birthday is in like three months."

"Yeah, I know. But we were going through old stuff to sell at home, and I decided to give you something. It was my first compound bow. It's not great or anything, but it'll work."

Maverick was shocked, "What? Willow! Are you serious?"

They checked out their equipment, which Willow had already brought and checked in for Maverick earlier.

"It's an SF Archery compound. It's what I used for a long time. My dad restrung it. You can adjust it between 20-70 pounds. I've got it set at thirty. I also got you some accessories, they're in the bag."

Mav smiled. Her mouth hung wide open as she held the bow and examined it. "Willow! I don't know what to say, this is so awesome! Thank you so much!"

Willow grinned widely and swayed side to side. "Let's try it out!"

***

Archer missed first period and pulled into the school parking lot about ten minutes before his second-period class. He—along with the rest of his siblings—missed all last week. He did sneak out of the house two of those days to meet Evelyn and give her a ride home. Besides last week, he'd missed several days, and his grades were failing—his parents weren't completely aware of those details. He had been working more, and school seemed like a big waste of time.

He sat in his car debating whether he should go in. He decided to go in and at least see Evelyn and Miles. Archer didn't have many friends at school. He just didn't have a connection to anyone there, but he didn't try too hard either. Despite all that, seeing Evelyn was worth enduring it.

He heard the bell ending first period and decided to get out of the car and head in. Like the middle school, attendance was at an all-time low. He found Miles talking to several other students he'd never seen before. Miles caught sight of Archer, "Look who's here! Lunch is a ways away. What brings you here today? Come for the walkout?"

"What walkout?"

"The walkout! It was organized by a bunch of people you don't know. I think there's over two or three hundred." The school had nearly 1,500 students. Archer hadn't heard anything about this, but how would he? He was never involved with anything school-related, even on social media. He'd just been focused on Evelyn, work, and the garden.

At lunch, Archer found Evelyn. She was pleasantly surprised to see him. "You know, you're not gonna graduate if you keep missing school like this," Evelyn said, trying to be stern, but she couldn't help but smile at him.

Archer lifted his shoulders, "Uh oh!"

They ate lunch together in the quad. Evelyn was talking about the ASVAB test she had to take at the Military Entrance Processing Station, or MEPS, in Charlotte. It was coming up soon. Archer couldn't help but feel a sense of sadness. He didn't want her to go, but she wouldn't hear that kind of talk against it. She would just say that they would stay together. She refused to talk about the details of how the future would look for them. She said they were meant to be. She could be quite romantic and melodramatic.

Sure enough, at the end of lunch, a large gathering formed in the quad with students. Several hundred teenagers were holding up signs and starting to chant several slogans. The students milled about. It was not anything organized by any means. Some signs said, *We need food not school,'* and *We have no future.'* Several orange signs and flags bearing the distressed crown were waved in the air as the students shouted and cheered.

Evelyn growled, "I can't believe this. They don't know what they're talking about. Did anyone attend history class? Do they know how many people died in the Civil War?"

They began to slowly walk around in a circle, chanting "No food, no school. No food, no school…" More and more students were joining in. Rocks and bottles started to be seen flying across the quad at the building and windows. Within several minutes, a police car showed up, then another. Orders to disperse mixed with whining sirens echoed throughout the quad. The chanting got louder and louder. The crowd started to spread. Archer could see Miles holding a distressed crown flag and waving it above his head.

Archer started to feel uneasy. Evelyn was shouting at many of them and he held her waist, trying to restrain her. A loud crash from a window breaking set off a roaring cheer and loud whistles.

"Alright, that's it." Archer took Evelyn's hand and started to walk out to get to his car, pulling her with him as she continued to shout back at the protesters.

The parking lot was now blocked by several police cars. Several officers started to group up together and slowly walk onto the campus. The crowd started to disperse as students started walking in every direction. Most started to walk off the campus. A police car with flashing lights and a blaring siren slowly rolled onto the quad, sending students scampering away in every direction.

Archer and Evelyn got into his car and started it, as had many other students who drove. Many of the cars were lining up at the blocked exit. Archer drove toward the rear of the school where students were throwing bricks and rocks. He saw several officers start to give chase.

Archer noticed an officer yelling at him in the car, all while holding and pointing a baton at him. "Turn off your car and get out—"

Archer hit the gas and drove his car onto the grass and was able to drive through a soccer field. His back wheels started to slide in the wet grass. He ran over a sidewalk onto the main road to make his escape. Evelyn screamed and covered her eyes the whole way onto the street.

***

Lexi had received a text from Stan about a grocery store near downtown Gastonia that had just received a shipment of ground beef. The timing was perfect as she'd just picked up Blaze from school, and Leo was with her as well in the back seat. She wasn't far from the store. She figured with traffic, she could probably make it there in about fifteen to twenty minutes. She was unfamiliar with the store—Henry's Market. The location was run down and wasn't in the best part of town, which made her a little nervous. However, the idea of having ground beef sounded too good to pass up. They also had to watch their budget for grocery shopping. Credit cards were maxed out, and their savings were all but gone. Luckily, Stan had just gotten paid, and she had some cash available right then.

She entered onto the freeway to give it a try and decided that she would check what the parking lot looked like and make a final judgment call then. When meat shipments arrived, it would spread like wildfire on social media sites. Stan would find out first and there was often a solid twenty-minute window where most wouldn't know. Usually, forty minutes or so after his text, it would be too crowded in the store, and all the meat would be gone. This was going to be close.

She arrived at Henry's Market. It was in a dilapidated downtown shopping center in an old part of town with brown brick buildings made during the days when textile mills flourished. The strip mall had a

Tobacco and Vape shop, an ABC store and thrift store. The parking lot was moderately full, but steady traffic was filling the lot. She parked the minivan and gave the usual instructions to Leo and Blaze to stay close, followed by the usual threats of timeout and losing their favorite toys if there was no cooperation.

Lexi held Leo's hand on the left and Blaze's hand on the right. She was pulling them along at an almost frantic pace. The kids were oddly quiet. They entered the store. Shopping carts were disorganized, and the cart corral looked like a bumper car arena at an amusement park. She pulled a cart from the coral and instructed the kids to put one hand on the side of the cart and stay close.

The shelves were rather bare, which was not unusual. They headed to the back of the store where the meat was located. There were several customers crowded around the refrigerated meat section. There appeared to be no limit sign, and people were tossing trays of meat into their carts. Lexi had to squeeze in and was able to grab two trays of ground beef. She attempted to grab a third, but a woman bumped her out of the way. As soon as she turned around, five or six more customers crowded in behind her. Two of them were yelling for everyone to save some for everyone else. A pushing match quickly erupted. A punch was thrown, and a man fell to the ground like a rag doll. Yelling turned to screaming. Lexi's eyes went to her kids who were getting bumped around.

Lexi dropped the meat and rushed toward them. She picked up Leo and grabbed Blaze's hand and ran toward the exit. The yelling and screaming were echoing through the store. As they got close to the door, three loud bangs that sounded like a sledgehammer striking a metal roof rang out followed by screams. Lexi wasn't fazed. She sprinted like she didn't know she could. Leo was bouncing up and down in her arms.

Leo screamed, "Mommy!"

She felt a rush of relief as she felt the outside air. She locked her focus on getting to the minivan. She opened the side door, and Blaze jumped inside. She tossed Leo in without any thought of the car seat and closed the door. Within a second, she was fumbling with her keys in the driver's seat and was able to get it started. She screeched out of the parking lot toward home.

Chapter Twenty-One

23 October

7 days before the war

At 8:00 a.m., nearly everyone would pause when the power came back on. It would stay on for two hours. Usually, everyone would be able to turn on their television, charge devices and check their phones for news and updates with Wi-Fi. On this day, all the reports were the same. A federal broadcast was posted with a message from the president, declaring federal martial law due to "widespread insurrection and imminent threats to democracy." In his statement, the president stated that Congress, in bipartisan agreement along with him, had made the decision after midnight. Effective immediately, the federal government would work directly with each state and even local officials to enforce laws to secure order. This included a mandatory curfew, the closing of all schools, national and state parks, etc. Public assembly must be approved by permit including for recreation, trade and commerce, and the like. The federalization of all state National Guard units was ordered as well. He cited the Insurrection Act of 1807 as the basis for his authority and called it Operation Friendly Neighbor.

While many states had enforced martial law over the past several months, this was the first time the federal government had ordered this since 1944, after Hawaii was invaded in World War II. The Governor of North Carolina had responded with a letter that was also distributed publicly. In this letter, the Governor refused to federalize the North Carolina State National Guard and refused to enforce martial law using

state resources. He also stated that he in no way supported the draft and urged all
North Carolinians to refuse to comply with the draft.

Calvin Eastridge made a written, audio, and video response that was posted
everywhere immediately following the news of martial law. It was pre-recorded as they
were ready for this to happen. In his message, Calvin stated that the militia did not
recognize the federal government's authority to enforce martial law and that all public
activity would continue. He also stated that the entire Calvinist Militia was in support
and at the disposal of the North Carolina State Governor.

Chapter Twenty-Two

9 June

143 days before the war

Winter and spring passed. The United States had ever-increasing rates of disorder and uprisings due to continued economic turmoil. Facing mass protests in the homeland, the United States was forced to abandon most of its support of European and NATO allies, as well as Taiwan in the east. American troops were slowly returned to the U.S. to curb insurrection and insurgency activity in several states.

The Deconstruction Movement exploded in the media and on social media. Everywhere throughout the United States, small militias to entire states with sanctioned military forces were threatening to revolt. Nearly 80% of the population was now on SNAP or EBT, which was formerly known as food stamps. The federal government had seized control of the entire supply chain to ensure that goods were distributed throughout.

In Gaston County, this was no different. Food continued to be distributed to stores, and a system was implemented for scheduling shopping hours for residents. As Stan predicted, this started with five windows per week that slowly reduced to just two at the beginning of June. People were hungry. Everyone in the Jenkins family had lost weight along with most others. Rolling blackouts were increasing in frequency and became scheduled to conserve power due to fossil fuel shortages.

The Calvinists started to become a household name within the county. They had sent a message of hope and provided security in the community as well as free training and classes for self-sufficiency skills. Their recruitment levels began to climb exponentially within the tri-county area. Calvin Eastridge and his message were growing throughout the community.

Picketing outside government buildings had started to become a daily event as people demanded food, power and jobs. The Calvinists took advantage and often either organized protests or would arrive at them to increase support for the movement. They had started several swap meets and locations for 'free trade,' where people could barter and trade, tax-free and without fees. They also provided security to vulnerable neighborhoods, often helping local law enforcement. In fact, many law enforcement personnel had joined the Calvinists themselves.

***

The school year finally ended. Evelyn had graduated a few days prior, and this was her last night before leaving for enlistment. On the roof of the Jenkins' house, Archer and Evelyn lay on their backs, watching the stars. It was oddly quiet. Most nights, sirens and occasionally explosions could be heard in the distance.

"It's not over for us," Evelyn randomly said.

"Yeah, I know," Archer said, feigning hope.

"Stop it, I can read your mind."

"Should I join the army?"

Evelyn laughed so hard she had to cover her mouth to keep from waking up the entire neighborhood.

Archer was a little insulted, "What? Why are you laughing?"

Evelyn pinched his cheek, "You're so adorable, you know that? You're not a military kind of guy. You're too defiant, too free-spirited. That's what I love about you."

Archer pulled away and pouted, "I think I could do it."

"Awe, of course you could, sweetheart," Evelyn said mockingly.

Archer took a deep breath. "I just don't want anything to happen to you. There's war everywhere, and I'm scared you're… You know."

"Going to die?"

"Yeah, going to die."

Evelyn turned to face Archer. She put her hand on his cheek. "I love you, but there's something bigger than us that has to happen to change what's going on in the world. I need to be part of that change, Archer."

That resonated with Archer. He couldn't think of a response. He stared into her eyes and ran his fingers through her long hair. "It's just not fair."

Evelyn smiled, "That's right! It isn't fair. We'll look back on high school and talk about protests and vandalism. How there were no sports, no prom, nothing."

Archer smiled. "No prom. That's right. Which don't get me wrong, it's not quite my thing anyway."

"Of course not, Mr. Too-cool-for-school."

Archer stood up and looked at his phone. "I have probably less than one percent power left, but I think we should go ahead and have your prom right now."

Evelyn couldn't stop laughing. "You're so corny, don't even do this to me."

"Oh, it gets better. It's going to be a song that's appropriate." An old, slow Elvis song started to play from his phone.

"You've got to be kidding me, stop it."

Archer held out his hand in a dramatic posture. Evelyn slapped his hand away, but Archer insisted. She took his hand and stood up. She put her arms around his neck, and he placed his around her waist. They slowly and awkwardly waddled left to right. Neither had ever danced before. Several small explosions flashed in ,the skyline. "See, we even have fireworks." The laughter soon faded as they stared into each other's eyes.

The phone died, leaving only the sounds of crickets and cicadas. They continued to awkwardly dance and kiss.

Hours later, Evelyn had left for boot camp, and she was gone.

Chapter Twenty-Three

24 October

6 days before the war

Stan had received a text message from Brenda early in the morning. He was just about to pull out of the driveway and head into work at the clinic.

The message stated, 'And I'm not sure what I should do.'

Brenda had a habit of sending multiple short text messages in succession, so he knew some of the other messages hadn't come through yet. He started to worry that maybe she was being questioned or harassed by Mr. Fredrickson and Agent What's-his-name. He decided to swing by the county building before going into the clinic to see if she was there. On his route, he saw several military vehicles on the road, which was rare for the area.

Down the road from the building, he could see several military Humvees in the parking lot. As he pulled in, he saw several county employees, including Brenda, outside talking to several people in uniform. He put his revolver in the glove box and exited the car to find out what was going on.

"I don't understand how you can do this," He heard Brenda yelling at two men in military fatigues. One of them, an older man with two black bars on the collar of his army combat uniform, stood with a calm demeanor as more employees behind him exited the building carrying boxes from their offices.

He spoke with a deep, loud voice, "Ma'am, we are taking this building in accordance with Operation Friendly Neighbor and need all of you to leave immediately. You have 28 more minutes to leave the premises, or you'll be arrested for trespassing."

Brenda was fuming. As she started to give the captain another earful, Stan gently grabbed her arm, making her jump, "Stan! You would not believe what's going on here."

Stan was speaking slowly and calmly, gently pulling her away from the soldiers. "Alright, let's go over here and talk in private."

Brenda started pacing back and forth, "I haven't heard anything about any of this from the county commissioners. I don't know what we're supposed to do. Are we fired? Have they just taken over day-to-day operations or something?"

Stan felt like he was in a therapy session. "Okay, just take a deep breath. What happened?"

Brenda paused and took a deep breath. "I got here at about 7:45 a.m. this morning. Rick, Tom, Wendy and a few others were already here waiting for me to arrive. I opened the building, and we went inside. Like exactly at 8:00 a.m., we see these trucks pulling up and a bunch of soldiers get out. That guy I was talking to says he's in charge. He said they're with the 3rd Infantry Division from Georgia. They're here to enforce martial law. But they told us we all had to leave the building, I don't know what we're going to do. I guess we're out of a job. I can't get through to any of the commissioners to find out, and I haven't heard anything from anyone."

Stan was worried that Brenda was going to refuse to leave and end up getting arrested. He talked in a slow, calming voice, "Brenda, just go home and keep trying to call. I wouldn't stay here. You don't need to end up getting arrested for some misunderstanding."

Brenda was shaking her head. She was fuming. Stan had seen this face and body language before many years ago when he worked under her. She looked at her phone. "You're right. I need to get some things from my office. Just in case I can't come back."

"Brenda, I think you should just leave. Whatever pictures or plants or—"

"Stan," she interrupted, "I need to get a flash drive that's in my office. I need it and I don't want them to have it or see what's on it."

"They probably won't even look."

"I can't take that chance. I'll explain later, but I need to get that drive."

Stan reluctantly nodded. He didn't like the sound of this, and his mind quickly wandered into all the worst-case scenarios Brenda may have gotten herself into. "Okay, we've got a few minutes left. I'll go with you."

Stan and Brenda walked up to the front door where the captain was barking orders at several soldiers as they carried in crates of equipment. The captain caught sight of Brenda and Stan approaching and gave an annoyed, exasperated look.

Brenda could see his face and preemptively spoke before the captain could. "I'm leaving, I just need to get some personal items from my office first."

The captain grimaced, looking at his watch, "And who are you?" He said directed at Stan.

Stan started to answer, but Brenda interrupted, "He's one of the LEPC members for the county and has some belongings here as well in my office."

Stan wasn't certain that the captain knew or even cared what the LEPC was, but he could tell the captain was suspicious.

The captain yelled, "Corporal Reyes!"

"Sir!" Came a voice from the parked Humvees. He jogged over toward them.

"Escort these two to their office to pick up their personal effects. Personal effects only! All the equipment and tech stays." Corporal Reyes affirmed the order and held out an arm for Stan and Brenda to follow.

They entered the lobby. Several tables with stacked boxes and computer equipment were being set up in the center of the room. Chairs and sofas were all stacked in the corner. Two soldiers were shuffling through the lobby desk and pulling computers apart.

"It's this way." Brenda nervously said as she shot a look to Stan. She had tried to mouth something to him, but he didn't pick it up. "It's right here." She and Stan walked into the office with Corporal Reyes behind them. Brenda went to her desk and stood over it. Reyes watched her closely. She started to take picture frames and stack them. She opened a drawer to her desk, and Corporal Reyes walked closer, peering down to see what she was taking.

Stan was nervous. He didn't know what she had on the flash drive, but it sounded important. He had an idea.

Stan darted to the door and shouted, "I'll be right back, I just need to use the bathroom."

Corporal Reyes turned 180 degrees, "Sir, get back here."

"No, I'll just be a minute, the bathroom is right here."

Corporal Reyes dropped his rifle into his hand that was slung over his shoulder and walked toward Stan. As Corporal Reyes started to bark at Stan, Brenda knelt down and pulled a flash drive from her laptop. She quickly reached into her shirt and tucked the flash drive into her bra.

"Stan," Brenda interjected, "Just wait a second, I'm almost done."

Stan held his hands up, "Okay, okay. I'm sorry, I just need to go when I need to go. Bladder problems, old age, all that."

They walked out as Stan helped carry a large house plant and Brenda had several picture frames and nick knacks. The captain eyed them suspiciously as they exited the building and walked out to their cars. Stan waited and followed close behind Brenda's car after she pulled out of the parking lot. After she turned at the first stoplight and drove past several blocks, he flashed his headlights at her from behind. Brenda got the message and pulled into an empty parking lot of an abandoned car dealership. Stan exited his car and walked up to the passenger side of Brenda's car. He heard the door unlock. He climbed into Brenda's SUV and shut the door.

"Okay, what was all that about? Why did I almost get shot by a teenager for pretending I had to go to the bathroom?"

Brenda reached in her shirt and withdrew the flash drive. "This has some information that's not on the server or anywhere else."

"Like what?"

"Contractor information mainly. Personal information for contractors we hired."

"What's the big deal?"

"Over the summer, after we implemented the food distribution schedule, we needed security at the grocery stores, med clinics and hospitals."

"And?"

"Well, we used the 6th Brigade."

"Are you serious? The Calvinists?"

"They were extremely reliable and very inexpensive. Half the state legislature and the Governor himself love them. They're close with the commissioners, too. This drive has all the names of individuals who worked for us. There're a few hundred local people."

Stan shook his head. "I have a feeling that little flash drive is not the only place where that info is stored. At any rate, I don't know what the big deal is. Questionable judgment, maybe, but you did nothing illegal."

Brenda shook her head. "To answer your question, this is the only place that info is stored. There are invoices on the server, but no names. I didn't want this falling into their hands and jeopardizing their identity. I don't know what the federal government is going to do, and I don't want their lives at risk on my part."

Stan was obviously annoyed, "I mean, why would you leave that in the office in the first place? Especially with that Fredrickson guy snooping around."

"It's the safest place. My office has a different lock and I'm the only one with the key."

Stan huffed, "I don't know. They were in the building by themselves when they questioned me the other day."

"I knew they were there. They questioned everyone. I need to keep this safe," Brenda said, looking around outside. "Any ideas?"

Chapter Twenty-Four

12 July

110 days before the war

Like most mornings, Reese was usually the first to get up, well before the power turned back on at 8:00 a.m. She had a very structured routine that the whole family started to rely on. In the living room, Reese managed a large dry-erase board. She had a schematic map of all the garden beds and listed what was in each along with important dates and deadlines. She had a weekly schedule for each family member and wrote their daily chores for the day pertaining to the garden.

This used to result in grumbling, but not anymore. The importance of the garden was clear. Everyone had shrinking waistbands, and everyone appreciated and prioritized the food they were growing. Reese kept order and, nobody argued with her anymore. She had patience and didn't overreact to every little problem like everyone else did. She'd grown her skill and knowledge over the last year and seemed to always be right. Now, at the age of thirteen, Reese was well respected in the neighborhood. She had an outstanding ability to set up and make complicated trades for bartering that often involved multiple parties trading items back and forth.

Lexi came downstairs as she was usually the second one out of bed. She made coffee right away, one of the basic staples they were able to obtain on their scheduled shopping days using EBT. Reese had started drinking black coffee as well, in fact, black was the only way to take it anymore as milk or cream were hard to come by. In addition to coffee, they typically were able to purchase a little bit of meat, beans, rice, pasta, etc. The camping stove they had in the garage was put into service nearly every day now as the electric stove could only able to be used at certain times of the day. They used cash to purchase propane, fuel, salt, toilet paper and other supplies.

Winter and part of spring were very difficult. The Jenkins had to skip meals on occasion and Stan and Lexi would sometimes split meals. Since the start of summer and with the EBT being used for basic staples, the family started to have regular meals again and often healthier than their diets used to be.

One of the neighbors was extremely good at making soap. They had a routine trade set up to obtain soap in exchange for babysitting and occasionally produce from the garden. There were certain items that everyone was on the lookout for—12-gauge shells, 9mm and .357 or .38 ammo were becoming rare. If they were offered for trade, they would go for a hefty price. So far, the ammo hadn't been used except for practice.

Lexi poured two cups and sat at the table with Reese. Reese was looking at a canning book they'd recently traded for. Lexi peered over to see what she was looking at.

"Oh, I wish we could grow tomatoes. That first attempt was a disaster."

They'd attempted tomatoes by planting early, but the soil wasn't right and when the temperature rose with the summer heat and thick humidity, the plants wilted away.

Reese continued to read, "We can, it's just hard with how humid it is and even if they make it, it's hard to keep the bugs off of 'em. I'm thinking we can grow some inside, maybe. We might be able to. I just wish we had more shade. When's Archer's last day of work?"

Lexi sipped her cup. "It was last night. The hardware store is closed down for good."

"We might be able to make our own soil mixture that could work for some big pots. We'd have to keep it moist, and move them in and out of the house. They need like eight hours of direct sunlight. The rest of the time, we could leave them in the dining room."

"I'm willing to try if you think it will work." Lexi smiled. She was extremely proud of Reese. She'd changed so much. She was more assertive and confident for sure but didn't seem to smile much anymore. This surprised her somewhat. Over the past year, Reese's acne had been fading away, and her face had been mostly clear. Lexi thought she'd be ecstatic, but Reese didn't even seem to notice or care.

Reese was studying her dry erase board and getting ready to write up the daily tasks. She also had the grocery store schedule listed on there as well. "Are you going to the grocery store today?"

"Your dad is. I've got a meeting with *'The Neighbors.'* I was going to tell you. That's going to be a regular weekly meeting, so we can put that on the board."

***

Archer woke up just before 8:00 a.m. He'd been sleeping a lot more than usual. He missed Evelyn and was hoping to get a letter or something by now. He had to remind himself she'd only been gone for ten days. It felt like ten months. Losing his job at Screws and Planks didn't help either. He lay there thinking that he had nothing to do and didn't like that feeling one bit. He sent a text to Miles, but it failed to send. After a couple more attempts, he gave up. Archer rolled out of bed and headed downstairs.

Lexi and Reese were still at the kitchen table, talking. Archer headed straight for the coffee pot.

"Reese! I'm all yours today. Tell me what to do. I need to stay busy."

Lexi finally saw the smile on Reese's face that she'd been missing.

"Really?" Reese beamed.

"Yep! I don't want to sit here with my dumb brain thinking and feeling all day."

Reese shuffled through her stack and withdrew her notebook. She thumbed through several pages. "The Allens over on Porter Trail Road need help with a new chicken coop. The Cranes on River Row Road wanted some help tearing down a fence."

Archer waved his hand, "Yeah. Just write 'em down. I'll get to 'em all."

Lexi turned around in her chair to face Archer. She felt so bad for him, first losing Evelyn, then his job. "This is a good idea, Archer. I like what you're doing. Why don't you come with me to *The Neighbor's* meeting? You could definitely help out there, too. A lot is going on."

Archer nodded, "Sure, as long as I get out of this house, and can't you guys think of a better name?"

"Well, Bob was thinking the '*Forest View Guardians,'* Chuck was pushing for '*Security Team Foxtrot Victor'* or something like that. I think Linda—"

Archer winced. "Fine, *The Neighbors*, just leave it."

***

Bob's house became the temporary headquarters for *The Neighbors*. There were now over 60 volunteers. Many of the residents had more time on their hands as layoffs and unemployment continued to rise. It kept many idle hands busy, and several volunteers were very enthusiastic to participate and protect the community. The results were very positive. Break-ins were at an all-time low, and residents felt safe. They had 24-hour coverage now and had been using hobby drones to help provide surveillance.

Bob's house could now easily be spotted as he erected a tall antenna so the radios could cover the entire area with no problems and even radio outside for help if ever needed. Lexi and Archer walked over to Bob's house on Thornbrook Drive. The garage door at Bob's house was always open now as someone was working inside around the clock.

This weekly meeting was for the "team leaders." Each team leader was assigned to work directly with seven teams made up of roughly eight to ten members. Each team was assigned a day to be "on-call" in case an emergency happened, and they would be ready to respond for their assigned day.

"Hey guys," Lexi waved as they walked up the driveway. "I hope it's okay, Archer's here with me. He's got some extra time and just wanted him to see what's been going on."

Bob smiled, "Of course! How you been, Archer?"

Archer nodded and forced a smile, "Hi, Mr. Bob." The words came out as he realized he didn't know his last name. "Hello, everyone." Everyone knew Archer since he had been working one shift per week since the start last winter.

Several lawn chairs of all makes and models were set up in the garage in a semicircle. Archer sat on the floor next to the large table where Bob stood and usually conducted the meetings. With the exception of Lexi, all seven team leaders were either military veterans, in law enforcement or both. Besides the seven team leads, of course, Bob who mainly handled communications. His house served as the headquarters. Chuck, the old salty yeoman who took care of the schedule. Rand and Steve were there as they used their drones for surveillance, which worked extremely well and continued to be a necessity. They all got along well together, overall. Lexi couldn't help but feel out of place having no military or law enforcement experience. She was only a team lead because she had been responsible for getting the watch group off the ground. Bob would argue that it's good to have some diversity of experience and different professions involved.

"I'd like to direct your attention to our first order of business here." Bob turned around and pulled a blue tarp off a stack of several boxes. "What we have here is a donation, thanks to the help from Linda and Boyce."

Linda, who was sitting directly next to Lexi, smiled and gave a proud wave. Lexi couldn't help but think her woodland camo fatigues, combat boots, and tucked-in, olive drab T-shirt were a bit overkill. Linda was a 50-year-old homeowner at Forest View who had served in the Army and liked to tell people about it. Boyce, sitting at the very end of the semi-circle, was a deputy in the Sheriff's department. Both Linda and Boyce had made it known about two months ago that they had joined the Calvinists' 6th Brigade.

"There are 20 SKS rifles here and about ten thousand rounds of 7.62 surplus ammo." Bob continued while pulling one of the heavy, wood-framed rifles out of the box. "They're all in decent shape for surplus weapons. They were probably built in the 1940s." Bob retracted the bolt and peered inside.

Lexi became quite curious, "Well, that was really nice of someone, where'd they come from?"

Linda cleared her throat, "Last week, I was able to meet Calvin Eastridge at a training exercise. I told him about our security team for Forest View and mentioned that not everyone owns a firearm or has one that's adequate, like .22 caliber weapons and bolt-action hunting rifles with scopes and that sort of thing. He mentioned they had some spare arms since the Calvinists changed over to .223 and AR's last year. They've had these sitting around and taking up space, and he thought we could make great use of them."

Chuck gave an audible grunt and shook his head. "I don't know if we should be taking weapons from them. Donation? I think we'll be in their pocket is what that's gonna mean."

"They just want to help. They value self-sufficiency, and this donation is a recognition of our efforts." Linda was noticeably put off by Chuck's remarks.

Bob set the rifle down on the table in front of him with an audible thud that got everyone's attention. "Well, that's what I want us to talk about. Linda, I hear you, and I do appreciate the gesture. We could surely use them. We could keep them here locked up, and anyone can check one out on their shift if they'd like after they've been trained to use it. Also, Linda, to be fair to Chuck's point, this donation did come with a request. The 6th Brigade has been patrolling the river trail, and they do provide security in other areas as well. Quite effectively, too. They would like to communicate and coordinate with us."

Linda nodded. Boyce raised his hand, "I'd like to answer to that if I may. That's a no-brainer. It's for safety as well. That way, we don't end up spotting a patrol if they get close to the neighborhood and we mistakenly see them as a potential threat. Also, if we happen to have a threat in the neighborhood and they get chased out, we want to alert them, so they are aware. We communicate with other law enforcement agencies all the time. I think it's a safe idea."

Bob nodded in agreement. "I do agree with you on that, Boyce. I was thinking we could take a vote on what to do about these weapons and ammo. Should we accept 'em or send them back and say thanks, but no thanks? Anyone else have anything they want to say about it first?"

Chuck jumped in, "I don't think we should take 'em. I don't know about this militia. I'd like to buy into their altruistic mission which sounds really nice, but there's got to be more to this. An all-volunteer militia? How do they get funding? How dedicated can soldiers be if they don't get paid? And that's besides the fact that a private paramilitary organization is against the law."

Linda stood up and was trying to compose herself, she seemed to be visibly getting frustrated. "We need to get with the times here. First of all, it is true that a paramilitary organization is against state law, that is, unless authorized by the Governor, which it has been. The federal government and its military are spread thin. They've deployed in the Midwest and the Northwest, trying to guard assets and prevent secession. Our own state here has activated the North Carolina National Guard. They are just under ten thousand strong. Most of the state government is friendly or in direct support of the Calvinist Militia. Throughout the state, we are twice as big as the NCNG. If everything goes right, we are hoping we will be under the direction and command of the NCNG before long."

"That's crazy talk!" Chuck interrupted. "The federal government will never allow that."

"And what will they do about it? Sue us? Charge the governor with insurrection? How will they enforce that? We're helping to keep order. Crime is reduced where we're active. Look at what the 6th Brigade is doing here for Gaston County. The county hired us for security. I get it, 5 years ago, this would have been different. But today—today we are on our own, and the federal government can't help us. I say we accept their help and work with the Calvinists." About half the group applauded as Linda took her seat. Bob asked if anyone wanted to say anything else. He looked at Lexi who always seemed to be level-headed and was typically full of contrary views.

Lexi shrugged her shoulders. Everyone watched her, expecting her to speak. "I get it. I don't think Linda's wrong. But what if the federal government does respond? What if they end up sending troops like they have in Texas, Wyoming, Idaho and wherever else? Do we want to be on one side or the other? If, by chance, there is a war, I don't think we can go wrong with staying neutral."

Bob asked if there was anyone else who wanted to say anything. The garage was silent.

"Alright then. There's eleven of us. Let's do a show of hands. All in favor of accepting the donation from the 6th Brigade and sharing comms in the future. Go ahead and raise your hand." Seven hands, including Bob's, shot up. "All opposed?" Four hands, including Lexi and Chuck went up. Bob cleared his throat, "There we go. We'll keep the weapons and ammo and put them to use."

Chapter Twenty-Five

25 October

5 days before the war

A day ago, the Army 3rd Division had started to enter the state and set up stations in city and county centers from Charlotte to Raleigh for Operation Friendly Neighbor to enforce the federal martial law that was imposed several days prior. Surveillance drones buzzed night and day, and it was difficult to escape the high-pitched sound. The sound was getting on Maverick's last nerve. She'd been spending most of her free time in the woods on the bank of the South Fork River, but even there was no escape.

As soon as morning twilight made the sky purple, Mav was up and out of bed, jogging out to the woods to meet up with Willow. She took her compound bow and, for the last few days, had been taking the 9mm pistol Archer had given her. She'd been practicing shooting ever since Archer showed her how to use it several days before. The woods were becoming a more dangerous place. While Calvinist patrols were always friendly and often a relief to spot, others used the woods to travel as well when they didn't want to be seen on the roads.

When she reached the land bridge where the South Fork could be crossed, she spotted Willow who was standing out in the open. As she got closer, she saw Willow tugging on the trot line she'd run across the side of the river, crossing over to the land bridge tied on both ends by two pine trees. Willow often strung up the lines to catch catfish using nylon twine. Willow hated fishing and would never do it on her own. Mav figured her parents must have ordered her to.

"Good morning, Maverick! Have you come to save me from this? I'm ready to jump in and join the fish here in a minute."

Maverick jumped off the last rock onto the land bridge. She couldn't help but smile. She always felt a sense of peace when Willow was with her. "Why are you doing this?"

"We need protein. Fish doesn't sound too bad either. How's Reese? She still cracking the whip at home?"

Mav chuckled and dropped her pack and bow onto a rock. "Yep, she is. She's gonna be super mad when she sees I'm not there. I'm supposed to be canning when the power comes back on."

"Why do you do it? You're like, never at home anymore. Is it because I'm so awesome?"

"I don't know. I just feel closed in when I'm there. I don't have much to say. I don't know, I just don't feel good there a lot of the time. Maybe after Archer leaves, if he does. I just want to cry when he's around."

Willow nodded her head, "That's deep, yo. Only child here. Never had to worry about all that. Want to go check the traps? I think there's a—"

Both their heads turned toward the east as they heard several rounds of gunfire echoing. Willow dropped the fishing line and crouched down. Maverick did the same. The gunfire was close. They could hear shouting followed by more gunfire.

"Where's it at?" Maverick asked as she walked on her knees next to Willow.

"I'm not sure. Let's head to your side of the river away from it, though."

They picked up their belongings, and when there was a break in the gunfire, they ran across the stones to the western bank of the river. The gunfire intensified and sounded like there were automatic weapons. As they sprinted on the trail back toward

Forest View, they spotted several drones flying overhead, toward where the gunfire was coming from.

Willow and Maverick ran through the mouth of the trail where it entered the Forest View neighborhood and crossed onto the paved road. They spotted a pair of rovers that were patrolling the neighborhood and ran toward them to let them know. The rovers were already heading in the direction of the trail as they could hear the gunfire and had radioed in what they heard.

Within several minutes, the team scheduled on call for the day was at the mouth of the trail along with Bob, who arrived as well. All were armed with the rifles they'd acquired a few months back from the 6th Brigade. The team took up positions behind cars and other stationary objects for cover. Maverick and Willow were behind a parked van with Bob who was on the radio. A Calvinist patrol had connected with Bob on the radio and said they were being ambushed by an unknown number of gunmen in the woods and that they had automatic weapons. They were trying to get away and had been pinned down.

Linda, the team leader, ran toward Bob as she stooped low, keeping her head down. "We need to move in and help!"

Bob looked at Linda in bewilderment. "We most certainly cannot! They're outside the neighborhood, and we are not soldiers here, Linda. We don't know who's out there. It could be the Army for all we know."

The gunfire ceased, and the radio went silent. Bob tried to contact them back, but there was no response.

That evening, Bob had been in contact with the Calvinists and learned that their four-man fireteam had all been killed. No other bodies were found, but they did find hundreds of spent 5.56mm casings typically used by the Army's standard issue M4A1 carbine.

Chapter Twenty-Six

2 August

89 days before the war

Around 9:30 p.m., Archer and Stan crossed paths in the kitchen. Stan was searching through the bags of loose tea that Reese had acquired in a trade. It was more of an herbal tea, like peppermint and lavender mixed with a little black tea. Stan wasn't sure what it was exactly but was feeling adventurous.

Archer had walked in from a rover shift. He finished at 9:00 p.m., but he had to check in the rifle he'd used and got stuck talking to Bob, who can be hard to peel away from at times when he gets started on something.

Archer, along with most others in *The Neighbors*, had completed a crash course training on using the SKS rifle. The course included basic safety, stripping and cleaning, loading and unloading, using the sights and, of course, shooting. Archer liked the SKS except that it was extremely heavy. Over the past couple of weeks, Archer started taking a lot of shifts to get his mind off Evelyn. He liked all the walking and being outdoors. It was extremely hot and humid outside, and air conditioning was being limited by the rolling blackouts. Everyone had to get used to the heat.

"How'd it go?" Stan asked, shuffling through Ziplock bags full of dried herbs.

Archer dropped his pack on the chair. "It was alright. Uneventful for the most part, but we got a couple reports of seeing some guys wearing red hoodies wandering around. I mean, who wears a hoodie in this heat? Anyway, Steve and Rand are on the lookout for anyone like that. We get any mail?"

"Not today, I'm afraid."

Archer dug into his bag and pulled out a pistol. He ejected the magazine and racked the slide, locking it open. "Check it out! Finally got it today."

Stan dropped the bags on the counter and walked over. "Oh, that's right. CZ P-10? What'd you trade for it again?"

Archer looked up to the ceiling, "Well, let's see. My Fender Strat and amp, my acoustic, a pair of hiking boots I never used. Uhm, what else? Oh, a pair of Ray-Bans, a poker set, that old wooden rocking chair we had in the garage—"

"I was going to use that."

"The weed eater"

"The gas-powered one?"

"Yep. Uhm, also, you had an unopened bottle of whiskey."

"Okay, you should have asked about that one."

"You never drink, Dad."

"Well, I may want to start here soon."

Stan put the magazine in and racked the slide. He aimed at the wall and peered down the sites. "I like it. Is there anything left in your room now?"

Archer laughed. Stan set the pistol down and sat at the table. "How are you doing?"

Archer quickly answered, "good."

Stan tapped the table to get some eye contact. "No, I mean, how are you doing with Evelyn and all that stuff?"

Archer looked into his dad's eyes. He pursed his lips, "I'm… Good."

Stan rolled his eyes. "Alright, alright. Good talk." Stan started to think about what an awesome and amazing therapist he was. He got up when he finally realized his water on the stove was at a roaring boil. "Oh, you want some tea?"

"Sure. Hey, did you hear about a draft? I've been hearing about it all day and saw a couple of articles about it."

Stan felt a pinch in his chest. He had heard the rumors in the media and all around as well. He just didn't want to think about it. "Yep, yep, I heard."

Archer paused, waiting for more. "Okay, and what do you think?"

Stan loaded two tea infusers and placed them into two mugs. He looked at Archer with a big smile, "I'm… Good."

***

Stan went up to bed late. He figured Lexi was asleep. He opened the bedroom door and saw Lexi's face glowing blue from her laptop screen in the pitch-black room. He knew what this was and knew he'd have to talk about the draft rumors. Stan climbed into bed. Her face was fixed to the screen. He just waited.

The silence was long and stretched seemingly forever. He couldn't stand it anymore. "So, whatcha readin'?" Silence. Stan felt an urge to fill the silent void, "That bad, huh?"

Lexi closed the laptop. "There's a big push to get farmers in the state to stop taking federal subsidies and use the farmland for local trade."

Stan felt a sense of relief. Maybe she didn't see anything about the draft. Or maybe she didn't want to talk about it like he didn't want to. Stan extended his arm out and Lexi laid her head on Stan's chest. He could tell the farmland thing wasn't what she was worried about.

At 2:00 a.m., the radio on the nightstand came alive with three obnoxiously loud beeps. A voice followed. "Team 6, Alert. 2207 Thornbrook Drive. Three individuals spotted breaking into the home." Lexi rolled out of bed and grabbed the radio.

Seconds later, Archer knocked on the bedroom door. "Mom, did you hear that?"

"Yeah, I know. I'm coming." She was already dressed and just had to put on the shoes she had next to the bed.

Archer was ready and put his CZ 9mm in the back of his waistband. They jogged over to Bob's house. The garage was open as always, beaming light out onto the dark street. Bob stood holding two Rifles, handing them off to Archer and Lexi.

"Be careful! There's three armed gunmen in the house out there." He said before grabbing two more rifles for the next two team members who would arrive.

Archer and Lexi continued down the street toward Thornbrook Drive.

"Why don't you go home, Mom?"

"Oh, you stop!" Lexi snapped back.

It was very clear outside, and luckily, a full moon made the neighborhood glow. When they arrived a few houses away, they saw Phoebe and her husband, Charles, crouched behind a car along the curb next to the house. Lexi and Archer ran up and knelt down next to them behind the car.

Phoebe whispered, "There's three men who broke into the house. We spotted them down the road just as they were entering. I don't know what to do. I don't want them to hurt anyone inside. I don't think they know we're out here."

Archer peeked over the hood of the Honda Civic all four of them were crouched behind. Just then, four more team members were quietly pacing up the road in a single-file line. Lexi held out a hand and lowered it toward the ground. The team members crouched down and found cover behind another car on the road that was next door to 2207. Lexi held out 3 fingers and pointed toward the house, letting them know there were three inside. Archer could see the lanterns or lamps glowing inside and shadows going past the windows. They heard several gunshots, and Archer could see the muzzle flashes light up through the windows.

"What do we do?" Phoebe whispered loudly and was starting to panic. They heard a loud thud inside, then the front door swung open, and three men in hoodies and ski masks quickly exited. Archer, Phoebe, Charles and Lexi, along with the four other team members, all peered over or around the cars they were behind, pointing their rifles at the three men. Lexi shouted for the men to stop where they were and drop their weapons.

All three men stopped in their tracks and were completely caught off guard. They looked around and at each other. Two of them held up handguns and began firing without even aiming. All eight of the team members instantly started shooting back with their rifles. The three men

169

were instantly hit with several bullets all over their bodies and fell to the ground where they stood.

"You sure there were only three?" Archer asked out loud since there was no need to whisper anymore. "Phoebe!"

Phoebe pulled her head up from looking down the sights and looked at Archer. Her teeth were chattering.

"Are you sure there were only three?" He asked again at a slower speed. Phoebe nodded her head.

"Everyone okay in there?" Lexi shouted as loud as she could. Only silence. They stayed behind the cars. The three bodies on the lawn lay lifeless. Bob, Linda and two others arrived, running up to meet Lexi. Lexi explained what had happened step by step to Linda and Bob.

Linda peeked over the roof of the car. "Do we know who lives here? Names? How many?

Phoebe looked at Charles, "Isn't it the Morrison's? I don't remember if it's this house or next door."

Charles Nodded, "Yeah, this is their house. It's an elderly couple. Doug and Florence Morrison."

Linda checked the magazine on her AR-15. She touched her two spare magazines on her belt, making sure she could feel the rounds. "Everyone, stay here. I'll go in. Just make sure you don't shoot me." She clicked on a light that was attached under the muzzle and ran with her head and body as low as she could get without slowing herself down. She ran to the door and peered inside, then disappeared into the house. They could see her flashlight strobing through the window as she was checking the house. After several minutes, she waved and announced she was coming out. She checked the bodies on the lawn and grabbed their firearms.

"All right, come on out, it's clear," Linda shouted.

They walked up the lawn where Linda stood looking at the bodies.

She looked at Lexi, "They're both dead, upstairs. They were both shot in bed."

It took over four hours for the police and paramedics to arrive.

***

Lexi and Archer were still at 2207 Thornbrook where the shooting had taken place. They were writing statements and being interviewed by the police when they were finally able to arrive. Stan had been up since the night before when the radio call came in. He'd found out quickly that something was wrong when he heard the gunshots. He woke up Mav and Reese and had them stay up to watch their brothers. It took him over ten minutes to run there as fast as he could.

When the sun started to come up, Stan walked back to the house to check on all the kids. When he arrived and opened the front door, Mav and Reese jumped up from the sofa and ran over to find out what had happened.

"It's okay, it's okay. Your mom and Archer are fine. There was an incident down the street." Stan hoped that would be enough.

"Did someone get shot?"

"Did someone die?"

"Did Mom kill someone?"

"Was there a fire?"

It was, indeed, not enough. Stan slowly raised a hand to quiet them down. "I promise, everything is fine. How about we make some breakfast?" Mav and Reese exchanged confused looks.

"We're gonna eat breakfast?"

"Is there some gang out there?"

"Is anyone dead?"

Stan again held up his hand and was getting frustrated. "Let's just get some breakfast ready and start some coffee, okay? I promise, I'll tell you guys what happened."

Chapter Twenty-Seven

26 October

4 days before the war

It was the second swap of the week at the elementary school. This morning, Stan was put on supervision duty. He was able to get Mav out of bed and of course, Reese was already out of bed and writing the chore schedule on the whiteboard. Stan decided to leave Leo and Blaze asleep. He didn't want to deal with them this early without Lexi. Mav agreed to stay behind to watch them while they were gone.

Stan pulled the wagon with what they could muster to trade with and Reese was following silently behind him. He was hoping to find lime powder. They'd been using wood ash to put in the compost which was helpful, but they needed to find lime to add directly to the red clay to increase the nitrogen.

As they arrived at the school, they saw everyone outside with several blankets laid out on the grass. It appeared the gym was chained shut. They'd been used to meeting outside, which is what they did before. Using the gym was rather recent. Several drones had been hovering overhead. As Stan and Reese rolled their wagon up to the curb, Stan tried to find someone to ask what happened and if this was just temporary. Stan spotted an older man who was standing near the chained door holding a radio.

"Do you know what's going on? Is it gonna open later or something?"

"I think it was the police or the army or something. I let the Calvinists know."

"Wait, why?"

Tires screeched to a halt in the parking lot, instantly turning Stan's head. Two Humvees parked in the lot, blocking the entry. Several soldiers wearing operational camouflage pattern or OCP uniforms and armed with M4s exited the vehicles and walked toward the crowd. A sergeant walked into the center of the blacktop, trying to get in the middle of everyone.

"Attention, everyone!" The sergeant yelled in a deep voice. "You are currently trespassing and congregating without prior authorization. You must all vacate immediately."

The thirty or so people, especially those who had set up their belongings on blankets started to whine and jeer.

A loud diesel engine was quickly approaching and dropping into lower gears. It was still out of sight. Suddenly, a large M35, fondly known as a deuce and a half, decelerated and made a sharp turn into the exit road of the school parking lot. The truck came to a stop. It was spray-painted flat black and had several steel plates welded on for shielding. An orange distressed crown was sloppily painted on the side. Several men in all-black fatigues and orange armbands armed with many variations of the AR-15 rifle began to pile out of the vehicle. The Army sergeant started walking backward toward his men, who all started to take cover behind the Humvees.

As the men exited the truck, they spread out but kept their rifles shouldered. People on the grass quickly jumped up and headed toward the school building to not get caught in any crossfire. Stan looked around and noticed they were stuck between the building and the blacktop where there were Army soldiers at the south entrance and Calvinists at the north exit.

The Calvinists approached. One of them, wearing a black boonie hat pulled down nearly covering his eyes, stepped forward.

"We'd like to know what's going on here, Sergeant." He had a calm, slow but confident voice.

The sergeant looked down and spit. "We are here to enforce the law. These people are trespassing and gathering without prior authorization. They need to leave immediately or be arrested."

"These people are not violating any laws and have the right to meet for trade and commerce. We do not recognize your authority here, Sergeant."

The sergeant paused and stared at the Calvinist. Finally, he walked back to his Humvee and opened the door. He could be seen talking on the radio, but nobody could hear what he was saying. Everyone stood still. Nobody said a word. Stan looked at Reese. She didn't seem fazed. He started looking around for an escape route and noticed a chain link fence about 30 feet to his right, past the gymnasium wall. He decided to slowly move with Reese in that direction. He figured he could lift and push her over the fence so she could make a run for it if needed.

It felt like an hour had passed. The sergeant closed the driver door of the Humvee and slowly strolled forward.

"We will return to this location in one hour. If anyone is here, they will be arrested for trespassing and violating martial law in accordance with Operation Friendly Neighbor. That goes for all of you as well," he pointed at the Calvinists.

The Calvinists all started to chuckle amongst themselves. "I think you ought to consider your rules of engagement for Operation Friendly Neighbor there, Sergeant," said the soldier wearing the boonie. The group erupted in laughter. The sergeant threw up a hand gesture and all the soldiers retreated to their vehicles.

Stan didn't think twice, he helped Reese grab their belongings and he pulled the wagon toward the exit where the Deuce and a half was still parked with its loud engine rumbling. As they started to leave, one of the Calvinists looked at Stan, "Hey, you don't have to go anywhere. It's your right to be here."

Stan smiled and waved but continued forward away from the school. As they approached the house, Stan told Reese to get everyone up if they weren't already. Lexi and Archer were at the table drinking coffee when Stan came bursting through the door.

"We need to get ready, there may be a gunfight here in a little bit."

Both Lexi and Archer rose to their feet. Stan started to explain what happened at the swap meet after telling Reese to get Leo and Blaze up and dressed.

"What time did the hour start?" Archer asked while heading toward the gun safe in the garage.

Stan checked the cylinder on his .357, "Forty minutes ago. They said they'd be back and I don't know if the Calvinists left or not."

Lexi was still standing next to the table. "Are there still people there?"

Stan shook his head, "Everyone was starting to leave, but I don't think the Calvinists did.

Lexi was looking at Archer, who took the Mossberg and Glock out of the safe. He handed the shotgun to his mother.

"And what in the world are we doing with these? We need to get to a safe place and hide out of sight!"

Stan agreed with a nod, "Yep, let's just take these with us. Let's go to the downstairs bathroom. It's surrounded by other rooms. It's got an actual porcelain tub."

At a minute before the hour, the Jenkins family headed into their downstairs bathroom. They put Leo and Blaze in the bathtub while Reese and Mav sat on the floor in front of the tub. Lexi and Archer were able to fit fine, but with Stan, it got extremely cramped. Stan grabbed the shotgun and handed Lexi the .357.

"I'm just going to be right outside. I want to check if I can hear anything out there, and I'll be right back if needed. Don't shoot me."

Stan ignored Archer and Lexi's protests and walked out the door, closing it behind him. He headed toward the front door and stood out on the porch watching. He realized he didn't even think of warning others. He'd hoped others would be sure to tell as many people as possible when they all hopefully left the school. Stan suddenly remembered the radio on the nightstand. Lexi always left it there. It was turned off since she wasn't on a shift. Stan ran up the stairs, snatched the radio from the nightstand and raced back down the stairs to the front door.

He turned on the radio. The chatter was overwhelming. He was trying to make out who was saying what when cracks of gunfire could be heard in the distance. The cracks and booms sounded like 30 bricks of firecrackers all popping off at once. After a minute, the sound dwindled to occasional pops, then it went silent. Stan wasn't sure what to expect next. The radio came back on. The rovers on shift were close by and were the first to report on the radio what they could see.

The rovers reported that Forest View Elementary School was clear, and some people were remaining who had refused to leave. The smoke that was now starting to be visible in the distance was nearly a half mile away on Mills Road, the main road that led to Forest View.

After nearly twenty minutes of silence, Stan went back to the bathroom and quietly knocked on the door, "It's me, everything is okay." Everyone slowly and quietly moved to the living room and sat together on the floor. Stan held the radio and listened to the chatter for updates.

Linda and several of The Neighbors *had walked up the road to investigate. When they arrived, nobody alive remained. They learned that the Calvinists had set up an ambush a half mile away on Mill Road, where they waited for the army soldiers to return. They set up the ambush in a heavily wooded strip that ran parallel to the road, giving little opportunity for vehicles to escape. Linda noticed the tire streaks on the asphalt and assumed that they'd used the deuce and a half and other vehicles to block in the army Humvees once they had attacked.*

There were several dead soldiers inside and out of the Humvees that were riddled with bullet holes and shrapnel. The Humvees were shot up and littered with holes. One of the vehicles continued to smolder, sending black smoke billowing through the treetops. Linda counted the bodies and explained that all the members of both fire teams were dead. There were also several bodies of Calvinist soldiers in the tree line.

Chapter Twenty-Eight

9 September

51 days before the war

The shootout on Thornbrook Drive had happened nearly six weeks ago, but the residents were still quite shaken. Tension was high in the neighborhood. Many wanted to find ways to improve security. There was a lot of disagreement on how to do this, and several arguments broke out over the past weeks. With the formal HOA completely gone, there was no association or leadership for Forest View. The most structured entity was *The Neighbors*, but even they struggled to know how to represent what the community wanted. After much disagreement and arguing, *The Neighbors* had started to set up manned barriers on the two roads leading into Forest View to slow traffic so that they could get a better look at who was entering.

Lexi had asked Stan for advice on how to organize a community this size since he was the social worker after all. Stan suggested creating groups with fifteen homes in each group. Each group selects a leader however they want, and the leader reports for meetings and relays info back to their group.

Lexi had tried to get this working. It took several weeks to let each of the 350 or so families know what was going on. Questions flooded in that she was unable to answer. Over the weeks, many residents had said they wanted to work directly with the Calvinists for security because they had lots of manpower and resources and were doing extremely well patrolling the woods around the neighborhood as well as the local community outside Forest View. Not everyone agreed with this. Even at home, Maverick was expressing that she thought having the Calvinist patrols provide support was completely necessary. Archer and Reese were unsure, but Lexi and Stan wanted Forest View to remain neutral, fearing the government may later intervene and they didn't want to get caught in the crossfire.

After two weeks of long planning and hard work, Lexi, Stan, Bob and Chuck were able to notify all the residents using the rovers to plan a town hall meeting to discuss what to do regarding security and the Calvinists.

The day had finally arrived, and nearly all the residents showed up at the parking lot of the elementary school. There must have been close to a thousand people. Lexi didn't even think there were this many, but it made sense with over 350 single-family homes. The meeting was extremely disorganized and loud. People were talking and arguing amongst themselves. Bob had a bullhorn that he brought and started to talk, which mostly got everyone's attention.

"This is quite a turnout." Bob was sweating profusely. "We are here today to see if we can make decisions about ways to address security concerns. Specifically, we want to reach a decision for the following: do we want the Calvinists to send patrols in Forest View or keep them out like we have been?" Voices erupted in unison with mixed responses. "Please, please, everyone. I'd like for anyone to be able to take 2 minutes and be able to speak about this. I'm not sure how much time we can spend. I guess it depends on how many people want to speak. Let's get an idea, can you raise your hand?" About ten or fifteen hands were raised in the crowd. Bob looked at Lexi and shrugged his shoulders.

Lexi grabbed the bullhorn from Bob. "Alright, everyone who raised their hand, please come up here to me and get in line. Everyone, please be respectful and stay as quiet as possible." About ten people lined up next to Lexi. She looked at all of them and got stern. "Just 2 minutes, please keep it about security, okay?" Everyone nodded in agreement.

Several residents, including Linda and Boyce, took two minutes to give their arguments for or against allowing the Calvinists to patrol the neighborhood. Those who wanted their support talked about the shooting and what would have been for the Morrison's had their support been accepted months ago. Some talked about how *The Neighbors,* as a watch group, was undertrained and outgunned by those who may want to try to take what they have. Those who objected to Calvinist support focused on how the group was still considered a private paramilitary group and illegal. If those in Forest View collaborate, they could be targeted by the government should they try to intervene.

They decided to try to vote. Each resident had one vote. Some argued that it should be one vote per address, but others said that was not fair to larger households and households with members who were divided themselves. They decided to set up lines to cast votes. Several would record the address and how they voted. The process took nearly two hours. The vote was close, but the majority of residents decided not to allow the Calvinists to patrol inside Forest View.

Stan let out a sigh of relief and felt like they may have dodged a bullet.

***

As he'd done every weekday since Evelyn left for boot camp, Archer went to the post office to see if there was any mail. The last two weeks, there was nothing, but today he'd received a stack of letters and junk mail. He jogged out to the car and searched through the stack, dumping everything on the floor in front of the passenger seat. He saw an envelope with handwritten address information on it. He recognized her handwriting immediately. The letter was postmarked over four weeks ago.

Dear Archer,

I'm writing to you once again. I haven't heard any response to any of my letters. I'm sure it's the mail service, but I do hope everything is okay. Boot camp is almost finished. It's a breeze.. I think even you could do it. I'm excited to head to Missouri for technician training. The Army Corps of Engineers is less than 2 weeks in sight.

I've made a couple of friends here, but mostly just feel homesick. I miss you so much and even miss my parents. I only received one letter from them, and in it they said they've been sending letters almost every day. I hate this feeling and sure wish I had my phone. At any rate, I'll have my phone after boot camp and can't wait to talk and text with you again.

Rumors around here are really crazy. We've heard that some states are threatening to secede. Some here think we're being lied to and it's already happened. I don't know what to believe, and we have no official word. I'm going to keep this one short today, I have to watch soon. I'm not sure if you know what that means, but I can't wait to tell you about it, haha! I love you so much and miss you every moment. Please stay safe.

Love,
Evelyn

Archer checked the postmark again. "She should have her phone by now," he thought to himself. He checked his phone and his call log, but knew he wouldn't see anything anyway.

***

Stan drove alone to Charlotte in the evening. He was extremely nervous and thought about skipping the event but knew he couldn't. This evening, Stan was scheduled to appear at the Mecklenburg Board of Commissioners meeting to provide testimony and report on the LEPC findings and recommendations for Gaston County. Stan was quite familiar with the roads in Charlotte and was able to navigate pretty well downtown. He just wasn't sure if there were any protests or riots where he was headed.

"I think I'm going to take this with me." Stan pulled the Ruger out of the nightstand drawer which now had a lock installed. Lexi was sitting on the bed, looking at her laptop while the power and Wi-Fi remained on.

She looked up and nodded. "If that makes you feel better, you should." A year ago, she would have said he was crazy. He thought about how things have changed. "Just—don't take it in the building," she smiled.

"Yes. Obviously. Thank you." Stan snapped back.

Stan was surprised at how smooth the trip went into downtown Charlotte. It was like things used to be. He felt a rush of relief as he pulled into the administration building parking deck.

There was a crowd of suits and dresses milling about in the lobby, waiting to enter the council chambers. There was a heavy police presence with private security as well. On an LED screen, the schedule was posted. Stan was one of the last advisory boards to report. There were ten others before him, including several townships, water, community relations and small business. His hopes to be first and skip out were dashed.

Stan was usually very disinterested in these kinds of meetings, but heard how many of the township's reporting had been in much worse conditions than what his family was facing in Forest View. He felt like they were in a sheltered pocket compared to the number of fires, lootings, riots, and so on happening just miles away. When he heard the report from the Charlotte Water Advisory Committee about the numerous shutdowns in service, a new worry unlocked in his brain. He never even thought much about water and waste. It was just taken for granted.

The Charlotte-Mecklenburg Community Relations Committee was announced next. Everyone in the seats started to whisper.

Calvin Eastridge was part of the advisory committee and here to testify. He was sworn in and addressed the commissioners with the usual greetings. Calvin was wearing a black suit and black tie. He appeared modest and humble. Stan was a distance away and couldn't quite see his face but could see his bright blue eyes. "I'm here this evening to provide a current update on the state of community relations. I think it's an understatement to say the community is struggling. I'd like to start with housing." He shuffled his notes and slowly put on a pair of reading glasses.

"Homelessness is at an all-time high in Mecklenburg County as well as every other county in the state. Foreclosures are at an all-time high, and most others are unable to pay rent. The evictions are jammed in the courts, and law enforcement is spread too thin to even be able to serve evictions. Needless to say, most people who have homes go to sleep every night terrified they will at some point be kicked out. Unemployment is high, which I know is odd when we also have labor shortages in most sectors. The problem is that pay has stayed nearly the same while inflation has quintupled. People can't take those jobs, because they won't provide enough money to do anything with. So, workers are also terrified.

"Schools are shutting down due to a lack of attendance. State law for truancy had to be suspended, not only because nobody is there to enforce it, but also because it doesn't make sense to go to school right now. Paid childcare is unattainable since workers are priced out of receiving that service. Parents are terrified.

"As of today, nearly 80% of the citizens in Mecklenburg County are receiving EBT and otherwise would be completely unable to purchase food in the grocery stores. We are only able to purchase food at times scheduled by the government and have strict limits on nearly every product that is available, putting a huge strain on large families. Everyone who must buy food to survive is terrified."

Calvin set his papers down on the podium and took his glasses off. He scanned the panel, looking at the commissioners and smiling. "While I am here on behalf of the advisory board, I would like to talk about recommendations, and I'd like to mention the organization I represent, The North Carolina Guardians of Liberty. You may not have heard that name, as we are mainly now called the Calvinists."

"Mr. Eastridge!" A woman's voice from the panel directed into her microphone. "The subject here today is on the—"

"Mr. Eastridge is recognized, and it is his time to speak." The Chair in the center spoke loudly and interrupted the objection. "Please continue, Mr. Eastridge."

Calvin cleared his throat. "Thank you. I don't want to waste anyone's time, and I don't want to mince words. We've never seen suffering to this extent since the Great Depression, and I truly believe this is worse. The federal government has enslaved us and made us dependent on its food, water, education, safety, everything. They continue to keep us terrified and dangle the scraps in front of us to keep us compliant. The farms right here in this state are strung along with federal subsidies, we need food stamps to buy food and have no way to legally engage in any kind of commerce as goods have stopped flowing in.

"Rumors of a federal draft have emerged, keeping us more terrified than ever before. How much more can we take before we have pure anarchy and lawlessness? We are here to support the state of North Carolina. We want a sovereign state and citizens who can take care of themselves and their communities. I know what I'm saying sounds impossible due to the rules and laws in place. I'm suggesting we break the laws and create ones for ourselves. Look at what the people want. Over half of the state legislature supports us, as well as the governor. We are now over 35,000 strong and are working to join with the governor and the North Carolina National Guard. I know there are laws but understand that we are in a unique time and we need to be ready to change."

"The gentleman's time has expired." A voice interrupted over the speakers.

"Thank you." Calvin humbly said into the microphone with a bow. Over half the members of the gallery stood up and applauded.

Stan was last to address the commissioners and spoke to a nearly empty gallery that evidently came to hear Calvin Eastridge speak. Stan wasn't upset by this at all. He stood up and listed off the numbers from his report and provided the data on food distribution and the rolling blackouts.

As he exited into the lobby. He saw a crowd around Calvin. Stan walked past and headed to his car.

"Mr. Jenkins!"

Stan turned around and recognized Calvin's voice from the testimony he just gave. He saw Calvin emerge through a group of onlookers and walked up to Stan with a big grin and extended hand. Stan wasn't sure why he'd even address him. "Mr. Jenkins. Calvin Eastridge." He shook his hand firmly. "You look just like your son. Archer told me all about you."

Stan nodded, "Ah! Did he now?"

"I just wanted to make your acquaintance. I understand from Archer that your family has been learning to homestead and has worked to get your community on the right track for a better life."

Stan shrugged a shoulder and gave a bashful look, "Well, we're doing what we can. It's been hard. Terrifying as you say." Stan was waiting for an acknowledgement of his humor, but Calvin only responded with a nod.

He put his arm around Stan. "I do hope we have your support, Mr. Jenkins. We all need each other right now."

Stan smiled and gave a half nod. He shook his hand one more time, then Calvin made an about-face back to mingle with the crowd and reporters.

Chapter Twenty-Nine

27 October

3 days before the war

The overcast morning was a welcome sight. There hadn't been rain in a while, and it was needed to break up the clay and water what was left of the summer crops. Everyone was home and awake. It was late morning. There wasn't much planned for the day. It had been nearly 24 hours since the shootout near the elementary school. Nothing seemed to happen in response. Tanks didn't roll up and air strikes were not called in. Stan had pretty much stayed up all night looking out the window.

Earlier, when the power was on, they saw on the news and everywhere else on social media that the North Carolina Governor announced that federal troops had 5 days to leave the state. He also announced the North Carolina Guardians of Liberty were now under the authority of the North Carolina National Guard, with the governor as its commander in chief. The media and pundits railed at the Governor and stated that he had no authority to take any of these actions.

He was starting to forget about what happened, and the worry was starting to leave his mind when a sudden pounding on the front door startled him and caused a hush over everyone in the kitchen and dining room. They all looked at each other. Stan checked his revolver cylinder and walked to the door. He looked out the peephole. It had been covered. Stan slowly opened the door. Three army soldiers were standing in front of his door. The tallest in the middle spoke, "We are here for Archer Jenkins. Are you his father?"

"Yes, I am. What do you mean you're here for him?"

"We are here to escort him to processing, he's been selected to serve in the military."

Stan opened the door wide and his face soured. "Well, you're too early. He has two days left."

Stan could now clearly see the one who was speaking was a sergeant. He opened a folder and withdrew a white piece of paper. Stan noticed it looked the same as the draft notice they first received a couple weeks prior. The sergeant handed Stan the paper and said that Archer's induction date was administratively changed.

"Sir, we are going to enter the home and escort your son to processing. He is coming with us."

Archer walked up behind Stan who was still staring at the soldiers and blocking the doorway so they couldn't enter.

Archer put his hand on his father's shoulder. "Hey, it's alright, Dad. Let them in. We'll cooperate." Stan didn't want to move. Something inside him snapped and he felt enraged. "Dad, please." Archer's voice calmed him. Reluctantly, he stepped back and let the soldiers inside.

The sergeant handed Archer another sheet of paper. "You have exactly ten minutes to gather all those items on the sheet. Some of them are marked optional. If you're not ready in ten minutes or refuse to cooperate, I'll arrest you and everyone in the home."

Stan huffed, "You cannot arrest all of us. This is pure—"

Lexi walked over and wrapped her arms around Stan's waist and stepped him back, telling him to calm himself down. Archer had run upstairs. Stan started to grunt and was holding back tears. Lexi had tears flowing down her cheeks. She was caressing Stan's face and quietly shushing him.

"They can't do this," he whispered several times. He was in disbelief and felt paralyzed.

Archer returned with a small bag and several cards and documents. He hugged Blaze and Leo who were standing frozen, completely uncertain of what was happening. Mav and Reese were both crying and hugged him together. They didn't want to let go.

Lexi gave Archer a very long hug, which made Archer start to cry. Archer finally came up to his dad and held out his arms for a hug.

Stan nodded his head. "I'm so sorry, Archer. I'm so sorry."

Archer hugged him, "I love you so much, Dad. I'll be okay, I promise. I'll be back, we'll be together again."

Then, Archer was gone.

Chapter Thirty

30 September

30 days before the war

Stan walked out into the waiting room of the clinic to find his patient scheduled at 9:00 a.m. The waiting room was crowded. The entire building was, in fact, over capacity. Two weeks prior, the clinic was designated, along with multiple other small community mental health clinics, to provide basic medical services for Medicaid recipients. This covered over three-quarters of the county. Nurse practitioners and physician assistants would arrive for a few days at a time to provide services from some government-contracted agency or another. Overall, it was confusing and frustrating for everyone. Stan continued to provide therapy but lost his office which had become an exam room.

Stan was able to locate his client in the waiting room and started to walk her back to the break room that now served as his office. Privacy was not always attainable, but he had to make do. His phone buzzed. He clicked it off, noticing Brenda had tried to call.

The phone buzzed again and again. After the fourth call in a row, Stan apologized and excused himself to take her call.

Stan accepted the call, "You know this is actually my day job, right?" he said feeling extremely annoyed.

Brenda sounded like she was in a panic. "I know. We were just told that the Selective Service is enacting a draft for the military. I guess the president signed an executive order. Men and women seventeen years old and older."

Stan sighed and closed his eyes. "When is this happening?"

"Now! They're setting up a local draft board for our county, and I have to use one of the administrative buildings next door to the courthouse. I need to meet with them and let them in. They already have board members assembled and ready to go."

"Okay. So why are you calling me?"

"We don't have any time to plan. People are not going to take this well. It's being released to the media within the hour. Can you please help me talk with the board chair?"

"How am I going to help?"

"I need a member of the LEPC with me, can you please just come?"

Stan slumped over and leaned against a wall. He wanted to say no, but also wanted to know more about what was going on. He reluctantly agreed and she gave him the location of where the new draft board office would be located.

***

Mav was collecting dandelions, chickweed and wild onions in the woods. She hadn't planned to do that this morning, but spotted them on the way to find mushrooms and meet with Willow, which had become her routine. Mav usually kept the stems and leaves for home and gave the flowers to Willow. Her father loved making dandelion wine.

Mav met up with Willow on her side of the South Fork. They were not at all the only ones foraging in the woods. Out toward Willow's home, the area was more secluded, and more foraging could be done. Willow looked at her watch, smiling. Maverick noticed. "What's up?"

Willow replied, "My dad should be passing here any minute. He and my uncle are training some recruits, and they're going on patrol."

Within minutes, Willow and Maverick turned their heads after hearing what sounded like an odd bird call—two short and one long bird tweet sounds. Willow laughed and shouted, "tweet, tweet, tweet!"

Several armed men and women wearing black combat fatigues were strolling down the trail in a triangular formation, spread apart. Willow's father was amongst them and let out a hearty laugh. He held up a signal, and everyone seemed to relax and mill about out of formation.

"Hi Dad!"

"Hey Kiddo!"

Willow's father and another man Mav had never seen before approached them as everyone else in the patrol had taken a seat on the ground. Willow ran up and hugged her dad. The man next to her father was wearing a black boonie that nearly covered his eyes. His white teeth contrasted his scraggly brown beard.

"There's my Willow!" He said in a drawn-out Appalachian Mountain accent.

Willow immediately let go of her father and jumped up to grab him in a hug, "Uncle Cedrick!"

Maverick felt awkward standing there with a half-smile. Brett looked in her direction with a smile and friendly nod, "How ya' doing there, Maverick? You got some more of them yellow flowers for me?"

"Yes, sir." Mav felt her voice crack.

"How your folks and family? Everyone staying safe?"

"Yes, sir."

"Maverick, I'd like you to meet my baby brother, Cedrick. He's one of our platoon sergeants."

Cedrick stepped forward with a smile and tipped his boonie hat forward, "Well hello there, Ms. Maverick, it's quite a pleasure to meet you."

Maverick forced a smile and blushed, "Hello, sir." She couldn't think of anything else to say.

Cedrick took a couple of steps toward Mav and seemed to peer into her eyes. "You pretty good with that bow?"

Mav shrugged her shoulders nervously, "I'm okay with it, I think."

Cedrick smiled widely, "Well, I hope so. It looks pretty familiar. I think Brett gave that to me when I was about ten years old, then I gave it to Willow when she was about ten. Now it looks like Willow gave it to you."

Mav felt anxious. She wasn't sure if he'd want it back or would be upset.

"Well, I think that's perfect. It looks good on you. It'll treat you well if you treat it well. I think that makes us all connected, then, eh?"

Mav smiled and nodded. She let out a contrived chuckle.

Brett gave Willow another hug. "You girls be very careful out here. There are lots of people with ill intentions roaming these woods. Willow, you've got the radio if anything happens. We're setting up another listening post nearby. Use the frequency that's just for the four of us—you, me, Cedrick and Mom, okay?"

With a whistle and hand signal from Brett, the team quietly stood up and went back into formation. Willow and Mav watched them stroll down the trail out of sight. Willow turned to Maverick, "I'm trying to get my dad to let me join. He says I'm too young, but I think he's changing his mind."

***

Stan was headed toward downtown Gastonia on I-85. The traffic was horrible. He turned the news up on the radio. Sure enough, a report was made regarding the executive order to implement the draft nationwide. The reporter stated that local draft boards were being set up immediately to manage conscription and process appeals. Stan scanned through the radio dial to find more information.

He took advantage of his time in the car to listen to the news. Between spotty cell coverage and rolling blackouts, the car was the most reliable means of information. Talking heads on all the stations were buzzing about the draft. One commentator yelled that the executive order was illegal and would never make it through the courts. Another speculated that their plan may have been to act immediately and acquire as many conscripts as they could before the courts could act. Some suggested that the courts would likely be ignored altogether. Stan had enough and shut it off.

Traffic was at a standstill near the courthouse. Most of the government buildings were clustered together on two small city blocks. Stan was losing his patience. The opposite side of the road was just as congested. He had nowhere to go. Horns from other cars began to blare. He was behind a large pickup and couldn't see far in front of him. He could hear noises but couldn't make out what it was. Along the street and sidewalk, hundreds of people were walking and shouting, heading toward the courthouse.

The walls of the buildings along both sides of the road echoed with chants and screams. The cars were all stopped. Hundreds passed through the lanes of traffic walking between the cars. Loud bangs and shattering glass sporadically echoed. In the rearview mirror, Stan could see a long line of police officers in riot gear getting into formation. The line stretched across the entire street and the sidewalks. Stan turned around to confirm what he was seeing with his own eyes. He started to breathe heavily. A rock or brick smashed and shattered the windshield of the truck in front of him. Drivers started to either get out of their cars or jam the road further by trying to drive up the sidewalks, attempting to escape.

Stan caught a glimpse of a flaming streak over his car through his windshield. He heard a burst and looked back to see a fireball flash in front of the riot police as a Molotov cocktail exploded and continued to burn and plume smoke in the air. Stan caught a whiff of the gasoline and motor oil. He reached into the glove box, grabbed his revolver and put it in his work bag before he put the car in park and shut off the engine.

Stan shut the car door and realized he left his phone inside. Just as he opened the car door. Several successive *thuds shot out* from officers launching tear gas canisters into the air overhead in his direction. The crowd in the road began to run and scream. White gas was slowly rising and spreading from the canisters. A man with a bandana around his face grabbed a canister with a towel covering his hand and threw it back toward the officers. Another, standing on the hood of a car wearing a gas mask, was waving a large, distressed crown flag in the air.

Stan could feel his eyes and throat burn. He grabbed his phone and ran the opposite direction of the police against the flow of the crowd. Loud bangs echoed through the buildings as the police used riot guns to shoot bean bag rounds at the protesters. Stan ran head on into a protester running the opposite direction and they both knocked each other to the ground. Stan grazed his forehead on the bumper of a car as he fell. He got back to his feet—dizzy, he saw fireflies in his vision. He shook his head to get grounded again. The air was caustic, He struggled to breathe.

Behind him, Stan could see the line of police slowly marching in step in his direction as the crowd clashed with the officers. A Molotov cocktail landed between two police officers, engulfing them in flames. Stan heard their screams and began to panic. He ran into a store building where the glass of the large window had just been busted out by a metal patio chair. Inside, the air was breathable. Stan couldn't stop coughing and his nose and eyes streamed tears and mucus. He ran through the building and was able to find a back exit to make his escape.

Chapter Thirty-One

28 October

2 days before the war

Stan hadn't gone to work since Archer left. Nobody left home, and everyone had been quiet. Blaze and Leo would ask when Archer was coming home and neither Lexi nor Stan knew how to answer that question. When he woke up, he felt the need to get out of the house. He was waiting for a call from Archer and kept his phone close. He hadn't called yet. Stan was ignoring all other calls and texts including several from Brenda that seemed urgent. His heart wasn't into work. He hadn't even called the clinic to let them know why he wasn't there.

Stan put on the shoulder holster he'd traded for at the last swap meet. He hadn't put it on before. It felt and looked ridiculous, but it had to be more comfortable than using the waistline of his pants. He put on his green jacket and slipped out of the house. He didn't tell anyone and figured he'd take a quick stroll around the block.

Almost an hour had passed. He looked around at the neighborhood that now lacked the aesthetic value it once had over a year ago. Most front yards were turned over. A layer of red clay covered the asphalt now making the appearance of a dirt road. He arrived back at home and noticed a car in the driveway. His first thought went to Archer and that something may have happened. He jogged back to the house and entered through the door.

The living room was empty. He didn't hear a sound. He turned and walked into the dining room and saw Lexi sitting at the dining room table, staring at him blankly. Two men sat at the table with her. It was Mr. Fredrickson and Agent Sorenson.

Stan froze. Anger flashed through his body, and his muscles tensed. He went numb. He looked at his wife and back at them. He had an urge to reach inside his jacket.

"Please have a seat," Mr. Fredrickson calmly said, slowly pushing a chair out from beneath the table. Stan took a deep breath and grabbed the back of the chair. He snapped from his trance and slowly sat down.

"Are you okay?" Stan quietly asked, staring into Lexi's eyes.

She nodded.

Mr. Fredrickson cleared his throat. "We are so glad you could join us, Mr. Jenkins. Your lovely wife invited us in, and we have just been getting acquainted while we waited for you."

Stan looked at Lexi gritting his teeth, "Why don't you go check on the kids, honey."

Lexi stood up and walked away, heading toward the stairs. When she was out of sight, Stan inhaled deeply, "I don't know why you're—"

"Brenda Long," Mr. Fredrickson interrupted. His voice was no longer so pleasant, and his smile was gone. "Where is she, Mr. Jenkins?"

Stan huffed, "What? Brenda? That's why you're here?"

"Yes, Mr. Jenkins. We understand that you were one of the last to see her and were with her five days ago at the administration building."

Stan moved his hand to his pocket touching his phone remembering the missed calls from the night before. "Alright, I was with her, but I haven't seen her since then."

198

"Have you spoken to her on the phone or by text?"

"No. What's this about? You guys come into my house and scare my family with this mafia routine because you want to know where Brenda is?"

"She's suspected of treason, Mr. Jenkins," Agent Sorenson interrupted with a raspy, high-pitched voice, almost struggling to speak. Stan turned his head to look at him.

Stan was waiting for a punchline and started to laugh, "What are you guys talking about?"

"She is wanted for questioning, Mr. Jenkins. This is a very serious matter," Mr. Fredrickson answered. "We suspect that she has obtained restricted information and provided that information to an insurgency group."

Stan thought about the flash drive. "There's no way. She's a bureaucrat for a rural county. She doesn't have access to anything important."

"That is partially true. She had no privileged access, but we suspect she obtained it nefariously. We believe that she has obtained logistical data that could be used to harm the federal government."

"I don't understand. Brenda takes her job very seriously. You guys are barking up the wrong tree."

"I appreciate your opinion, Mr. Jenkins, but I need you to tell me her known whereabouts."

"I don't know."

"Have you had contact with her daughter, Kaylee Long?"

"What? No!"

"Why don't you try to call her right now, Mr. Jenkins. Perhaps she will answer."

"No."

Bang!

Agent Sorenson slammed his fist on the table. Stan was startled. Agent Sorenson looked into Stan's eyes. "I don't care what you think of the situation, Mr. Jenkins. We believe that Brenda Long has given or sold information on the exact locations of our supplies within the county limits—that includes food storage, medical supplies, and yes, weapons. She has information on deliveries, manifests, everything. Now, if you want to remain here in this home and you want your family to be safe, you will cooperate."

Stan's mind flashed a memory of being screamed at by a principal in fourth grade. His heart rate shot up, and he started to feel cold sweat and chills throughout his entire body. He swallowed. "I don't know where she—"

"Call her."

Stan withdrew his phone from his pocket. He pulled up her contact information to make a call. Agent Sorenson firmly grabbed Stan's wrist.

"I want you to call and put it on speaker. If she answers, tell her you need to see her and ask where you can meet."

Stan paused. He pressed the button and the phone rang. Stan felt like this was wrong. He prayed she didn't answer. The call went to voicemail.

Mr. Fredrickson handed Stan a business card. "If you see or talk to her, say nothing of this. You will contact me right away, yes? You do have a lovely family, Mr. Jenkins. Be mindful of their well-being."

After they saw themselves out, Stan remained at the table and stared at the card. Within a minute, Lexi was downstairs sitting with Stan.

She told him that she overheard what was said. Stan shook his head thinking back to the day at the office when Brenda took the flash drive. "There's just no way. She told me she needed a flash drive with people's personal information on it. It didn't really make sense."

"It sounds like they may be right," Lexi said cautiously.

"I can't believe she would do something like that, she's not a Calvinist."

Chapter Thirty-Two

29 October

1 day before the war

Archer woke up when bright fluorescent lights illuminated the room. He'd forgotten where he was. He lifted his head and saw the rows of metal bunk beds. The sound of eighty or ninety men stirring and groaning in their beds started to fill the room. Archer was still wearing the clothes he had been picked up in. He'd been stuck here in what seemed like a warehouse of young men, all *in processing* and waiting to be officially inducted to start basic training.

Males and females were separated into large groups. They were told nothing about when training would start or what was going on in the country, or world, for that matter. Over the past two days, the eighty men in Archer's company had nothing at all to do but wait. There were army drill sergeants who would frequently show up at seemingly random times to yell and keep order and get them in and out of line to eat three times per day. Some of the men resisted and made the mistake of trying to leave or argue with the drill sergeants. Throughout the long and boring days, sounds of crying and begging to return home could be heard frequently, especially when it was dark.

Archer kept quiet. He was scared. He missed his family, but part of him felt he was a little closer to finding Evelyn. He just wanted to know what was happening and how long he would be here.

After Archer stood up and stretched, he heard a commotion at the door. Two of the drill sergeants entered the room and were silent. A hush fell over the room. Typically, they'd be yelling at someone by now. They stood silent. A man in civilian business attire entered the room and stood between them. "May I have your attention?" the man called out. He smiled widely and nodded as the room fell silent and all eyes were drawn to him.

"Thank you. I want to thank all of you for your cooperation and service. My name is Edwin Mays with the Selective Service System. I know you have been waiting a long time, but I'm sure you can imagine that we have many of you to process in order to start your training in the United States Army.

"Today, you will be moved to what is called, *Reception Battalion* to officially begin your induction. There, you will be processed for several days to begin your basic combat training. I want to thank you all for being our guests here over the last two days or so. Please be sure to collect your—"

"Where are we going?" A young man called out.

The two silent sergeants came to life and charged into the boy's face, screaming inaudible words.

"Please, please!" Edwin Mays interrupted. "I know you all have many questions and your anxiety is high. I can very much appreciate that. You are here because your country needs you. We are fighting for our survival and the survival of the United States of America. Your training will provide all you need to know to accomplish this. Again, I thank you, and God bless the United States of America." Edwin turned around and walked away. The Sergeants took over and sternly barked out concrete instructions on how to proceed.

***

Lexi and Reese walked over to Bob's house, now mostly known as *The Neighbor's HQ*. Reese was coming along to help them can their vegetables since Wendy had asked for help. They were both quiet. Reese wanted to ask about Archer but knew her mother would just be upset. She didn't know anything anyway. The Sound of choppers seemed to come from everywhere.

"Where are they?" Reese nervously asked. Lexi scanned the skies and shook her head. "I don't know but it sounds like there's a lot of them somewhere. Let's just hurry and get this over with." They continued looking up in the sky the entire way but couldn't see anything. They were both feeling nervous and quickened their steps.

The garage door was open, and they could see Bob sitting at his station on the HAM radio. He was listening intently and writing notes. He held up a finger, requesting that they pause and wait for him. Wendy walked out to the garage and greeted them. She brought two jars in her hands with vegetables inside.

"Reese! I'm so glad you're here. I can't seem to get the lids to seal, and I don't know what's going on. They sometimes bend too."

Reese took the jar and inspected it. "Your lids are too tight. You want to leave a little space for air to get out."

Wendy had a surprised look, "Are you sure? Do you want to see the others?"

"I'm sure. I can help you if you'd like since we're here."

They started to head inside the house. Bob threw his headphones on the table. "I can't believe it! Well, we're in it now."

"What?" Lexi asked.

"The Calvinists. They just made a big, coordinated attack in broad daylight. All over the place. From Fayetteville to Charlotte to Raleigh. I'm trying to keep count. Here, they hit several warehouses in Gastonia where they were storing ammunition. Sounds like they either captured, raided or burned a bunch of other locations where the Feds were storing supplies. They did it all at exactly the same time. Sounds like they attacked the building where your husband worked at the county, too. They got half the 3rd Infantry Division on the run. Can you believe that? Well, so much for *Operation Friendly Neighbor!*"

Lexi nodded her head.

"I heard from a division commander I've been talking to. He said it was in response to an attempt to arrest the governor for sedition last night in Raleigh. Sounds like he got away, though."

Lexi was hit with a sense of hopelessness. She didn't know what to say and just put her arm around Reese and squeezed her shoulder. Reese looked at her mother who wanted to burst into tears. "It's going to be okay, Mom. Let's just go home."

Lexi smiled and nodded and tried to say yes, but no words could come out. Reese took her mother's hand and led her out of the garage.

Bob looked at his wife, confused, "What'd I say?"

Wendy clicked her tongue and snapped, "Bob, you bird brain. Think about what that means for Archer!"

***

That night, the power remained shut off even though it was scheduled to turn on. The Jenkins family sat quietly at the dinner table. The dining room was dimly lit from several oil lamps. They'd used the propane stove to make pasta and used sauce they'd canned several weeks ago. It was silent.

Stan looked at Archer's empty chair and paused his chewing. His stomach turned. Lexi hadn't touched her food and stared into one of the lamps.

"You need to eat," Reese said coldly to her mother.

"I know," Lexi replied.

Mav was shoveling food, focused and seemingly ignoring everyone else.

"What's gonna happen to Archer?" Blaze asked.

Mav had her mouth full of food. "He's going to go to war and fight. He'll probably die."

Stan dropped his fork on the table, "What is the matter with you?"

Mav shrugged her shoulders, "It's true."

"No, I mean it. What is wrong with you?"

"Stop," Lexi said with tears streaming down her face.

"You run out into the woods every day. You don't listen to anything we tell you. You talk to us like we're trash."

"I don't like it here. That's my problem."

"I don't care. You're still my daughter and you're going—"

"Stop!" Lexi snapped. "You both need to calm down. We're all hurting right now."

"What do you know about hurting?" Mav yelled at her mother as she instantly broke into tears. "You guys just sit here. You just try to put your head in the ground and hope everything is okay. You don't know how to keep us safe. You're just ignorant. You let people break into the house, and you let Archer just go off to die. You do nothing!"

Stan took a deep breath. Tears were welling up in his eyes. Lexi grabbed his hand. He put his hand on top of hers and took another breath. The anger was overwhelming him. "I know, you're angry. I am trying to keep everyone safe. I have five children to think about, not just one—"

"Well, we're not safe!"

In a rage, Lexi swatted her bowl of pasta off the table. The plastic bowl bounced on the tile floor, splattering macaroni and pasta sauce everywhere. "That's enough, Mavis. You want to know what ignorant is? It's you. You're a fourteen-year-old child who understands nothing about the real world. You're the one with your head in the sand. You run out into the woods to escape because you're hurting. You're just running away from us!"

"I hate all of you." Maverick stood up and stormed off upstairs.

Stan put his hand on Lexi's shoulder. He was now trying to calm her down. His emotions were all mixed up. What she said was true, and he knew they had to be able to talk about it to solve anything. Too much had been left unsaid for months.

Chapter Thirty-Three

30 October

Day 1 of the War

Stan jumped out of bed just as the sun was starting to come up. He forgot to set his alarm. He wanted to wake up two hours earlier to catch Mav before she left the house. He wished he could lock her in her bedroom, but that just wasn't possible or helpful.

He checked the girl's room. The beds were empty. He walked downstairs and didn't see anyone. He walked into the dining room and saw Reese outside in the garden. When he got outside, he could feel the chill. It was late October, and there was no longer a question of the frost. "Mav still here?"

"Nope, she left early. She didn't even tell me she was leaving." Reese was chopping wilted stalks and leaving them to fertilize the soil.

Stan felt his heart sink. He wanted to apologize and tell her how much he loved her. He looked at Reese who continued to swing the machete. He thought about her and how she must be feeling. He felt neglectful of her. "Hey, Sweetheart?"

"What?"

"I'm very sorry about how I acted last night and the things I said."

Reese continued to swing and chop away. The stalks dropped to the bed at a quick, even pace. "I know, Dad. I know you're doing your best. She wasn't being fair. She's angry and wants someone to blame."

Stan chuckled and was impressed at his daughter's insight. She'd grown so much, so fast and was no longer the shy, anxious girl she was. "Thank you. I appreciate that. I appreciate you and everything you do. You and your mom keep our house running and… well, I just want you to know, I love you."

"I love you too, Dad." She stopped swinging the machete. "You'll have to hug me later, okay?"

Stan erupted in laughter. "You got it."

***

Maverick was shooting her bow into a bale of straw that Willow had brought out over a week ago. She'd take advantage of any time her father let her take the four-wheeler and bring large items out to their meeting spot near the South Fork land bridge.

Maverick only saw Willow once since the Calvinist patrol was ambushed in the woods the other day. Willow's parents wouldn't let her venture out anymore, so she'd only be able to sneak out when her parents were busy. She wanted to see her.

Maverick noticed a jackrabbit hopping along Willow's side of the bank. She stood still and watched—slowly notched an arrow and aimed. She exhaled and released, sending an arrow right through the rabbit's abdomen. It jumped as the arrow hit, and the rabbit fell lifeless to the ground.

"I guess I'm just in time for breakfast?"

Maverick jumped in a startle. She looked toward the tree line behind the bank and saw Willow smiling and waving. Maverick smiled and laughed. She felt so relieved to see her. She ran across the felled log to the bank and gave Willow a hug.

"Whoa, whoa! What's all this?"

Maverick couldn't help but laugh. "I'm just glad to see you."

***

Lexi got the boys up as soon as she had gotten dressed. It was after 8:00 a.m. The power hadn't come on, and hadn't been on for over two days at the scheduled time. She went downstairs and saw Stan making breakfast. She headed straight to the percolator and filled a mug. "Did you talk to her?"

Stan was pouring oatmeal into bowls. "She was already gone."

Lexi rubbed his shoulder. "You'll talk to her."

She sat at the table watching Reese through the sliding glass door. "We need to get it together, though. We can't be moping around. These guys need us more than ever right now."

"I know," Stan robotically acknowledged.

"Are you going to work?"

"Not today." He turned to face her, "Just one more day. I promise."

"Well, we're making use of your day off, then. There's a list of *Stan chores* on the board that have been needing some attention. I have to go to the store today. We need it."

"No. It's too crazy out there."

"Stan, we need a ton of stuff. Look at the whiteboard! Reese's going to end up walking to Food Towne on her own if one of us doesn't go!"

Stan brought the bowls to the table and called over Leo and Blaze. "Fine, but I'll go. I don't want—"

"Oh no! I need to get out of here. You have scrubbing, assembling, and lifting to do here today. I'll be fine. I'm going to head out right now. This is the best time. The lines are short."

Stan rubbed his temples and winced. "Would you just take the Glock with you?"

"No, I'll be fine. Stop worrying."

Lexi stood up and took her mug with her to the door where she grabbed her bag and keys and walked out. She gave a big wave. "Get to work! I love you." The door shut behind her.

***

Mav and Willow had cooked the jackrabbit on a small fire they made. Willow skinned and cleaned it since Mav shot it. That was the rule. Willow stood up and started to kick dirt and stomp out the fire. "Alright, we've got a busy schedule. We have traps to check. I'm afraid of what we'll find, but I don't want to leave them out there."

Mav picked up her bag and bow. They headed across the log, toward Willow's house. Willow had marked the map. She planned to head north, two miles past her home.

The trail was calm and quiet. There wasn't a cloud in the sky. Mav closed her eyes and breathed in the air and took in the sounds of the birds and the bubbling river.

"Hey, watch where you're going." Willow quipped as Maverick grazed the back of her heel.

"Sorry, I'm just taking it in. I just wish I could live out here."

"Well, there are places you could stay. Though I don't recommend it. I found out from my dad that they've been digging tunnels and foxholes all over the mountains. I mean, I found out from my dad. He doesn't know that I know. Okay fine, I may have been snooping around."

"I'm not surprised."

"What's wrong at home?"

"Everything. I got so angry last night and said some terrible things. Especially to my dad. I feel horrible. I just don't know how to talk about how I'm feeling. As soon as I start, I just get so mad. I can't help it."

"I think I get it. I do think it's funny how I wish my dad were like your dad, and you wish your dad were like mine. It's almost like—"

Willow abruptly stopped and lifted her head, looking around. Her smile faded.

"What's wrong?"

Willow whipped her head around and looked at Maverick with a confused look. "Do you hear that?"

***

There weren't many cars on the road at this time in the morning. Lexi passed several businesses that had been vandalized and damaged. Glass shards littered the streets. The sidewalks were always busy now, and the streets usually had more bicycles than cars. She entered the parking lot of Food Towne USA. A burned-out Humvee sat in the center of the lot.

People were inspecting and scavenging inside it. An NCNG Humvee was parked beside it. Several Calvinists and NCNG were now replacing federal troops at store locations to provide security.

She parked as close to the front of the store as she could. As she exited, she looked across the street at an orange distressed crown flag waving in the wind outside what appeared to be an old feed store and warehouse. Several armed Calvinists in their black fatigues were walking the perimeter.

She checked her wallet to make sure she had the proper cards and credentials to get inside. In the distance, she heard what sounded like thunder. She looked up, but there wasn't a cloud in the sky. Nothing. The thunder continued to roll. It didn't sound like jets or even drones. The troops in the Humvee started to shout. She tried to make out what they were saying. Suddenly, a missile screeched overhead in the blink of an eye, trailing a thunderous wave that shook all the windows. Several more flew over at varying altitudes all heading northeast.

***

Stan was watching Leo and Blaze run through the garden, screaming and laughing. Reese was transferring compost from the bin to the wheelbarrow.

"I told you I was going to do that," Stan said with a pinch of guilt.

"I know, I got tired of waiting."

"You know, you've got a way of saying things without saying them." Stan stood up and stretched his arms. He walked over to Reese. "A little patience is all I'm asking for. Give it here."

Reese handed the pitchfork to her dad, "When I ask people, they just say words. They don't do what they say they will."

"Ouch."

"If you're going to do it, then do it. If not, just give me the pitchfork."

Stan continued to dramatically stretch his arms and torso. "I am going to do this right now, boss. There is nothing in the world that will get in my way, and I will not stop until it is complete."

"More words."

Stan took the pitchfork and stabbed it into the compost pile. Distant thunder started to roll. Stan and Reese started to look up in the sky as it got louder and louder. "That sounds odd," Stan said nervously. Reese called out for Leo and Blaze. Stan slowly spun around looking up in the sky, trying to figure out where the sound was coming from.

Missiles began to screech overhead. Reese grabbed Leo and Blaze and pulled them close to her.

"Get in the bathtub!" Stan yelled.

Reese kept her arms around both boys, pushing them toward the door. Stan dropped the pitchfork and ran to the side of the house to get on top of the roof as rockets screamed past heading toward the foothills and woods. Stan could feel the house trembling as they passed overhead.

When he reached the roof, he heard sirens starting to wail—the sirens used when tornadoes were expected. From the top of the roof, he could see downtown Gastonia and the Charlotte skyline.

In all directions, silent plumes of fire and black smoke started to rise in seemingly random locations over the entire county. Seconds later, the silence was broken with deafening booms that shook the ground. He looked toward Gastonia, then toward the woods. Just as his brain pictured the faces of his wife grocery shopping downtown and Mav running through the woods, a missile flew fifty feet overhead and slammed into a single, two-story house about two blocks away. The exterior of the house remained surprisingly intact, but the windows and doors burst out flames and glass. The boom from the explosion sent a visible shockwave in all directions. Anything glass instantly shattered. Stan felt a pulse through his body that pushed him off his feet onto the roof shingles.

***

Willow took the handheld radio that her father gave her out of her pack as missiles were screeching overhead. Mav was looking up at the sky. "What do we do?"

Willow paused, holding the radio, "Uh, I don't know. I got to tell my dad and Cedrick where we are. He's gonna kill me." Willow radioed her father, telling him their location. Mav walked off the trail to a nearby boulder where she could climb up and get a better view.

Missiles screamed by, slamming into the distant hills and mountains. Willow noticed Mav standing on top of the boulder, "Hey, get down from there! We need to get low and take cover."

Maverick turned around to face her. She pointed toward the mountains, "It's like they're just hitting certain places all over. I don't get why—"

Boom!

About a hundred yards away, a missile shot into the earth, sending an exploding bubble of dirt, trees and brush from where it landed. The shockwave pulsed, pushing Maverick off her feet as she tumbled off the boulder to the ground below. She landed face-first, hitting her head on the ground. Willow was mostly shielded by the side of the boulder, but still got knocked over to the ground. Willow looked to see Mav beside her, lying face down. Rock, dirt, and chips of branches and tree trunks rained down on them. Willow leaped at Mav and covered her head with her body.

Seconds later, the rain of debris stopped. Willow could only hear a loud ringing. "Oh no, oh no, Mav!" She yelled, hearing her own muffled voice.

***

Lexi looked behind her toward the grocery store building. People were filing out the front door, looking up at the sky. The tornado sirens started to blare. Distant booms in all directions sent a panic through the gathering crowd in the parking lot.

The NCNG troops were running toward the crowd, screaming, "Everyone get down, everyone get—"

Boom!

About a hundred yards away, the feedstore warehouse exploded, lifting the entire metal roof off the structure. The mortared bricks all shattered and flew in every direction. The three Calvinist soldiers were engulfed by the fireball.

The shockwave knocked every standing person flat to the ground while the front glass wall of Food Towne and every car window in the parking lot exploded into shards in unison. Lexi's minivan was between her and the blast, which helped to shield her, but she was peppered by the broken glass from her car windows as she fell to the ground.

She opened her eyes and saw the sky. It was silent. Her ears started to ring. She was in a daze. It was fuzzy. Time and space were incomprehensible to her at that moment.

***

Willow rolled Mav over onto her back. Her eyes were closed, and her face and body were covered in dirt. Blood streamed from a cut on her forehead. Willow couldn't catch her breath. She kept calling her name, but Mav wouldn't respond. She put her head to her chest, then her hand to her nose and mouth. She could feel her breath. Willow let out a loud grunt in relief. She gently slapped Mav's face and turned her head. Mav's eyes opened and looked around, then closed again.

Several missiles continued to roar overhead, flying over the foothills toward the mountains. Willow started to cry. She held onto Mav, wiping the dirt from her face.

"Think this is bad? Wait 'til your daddy gets a hold o' you!" Willow whipped her head around and saw Cedrick running toward them.

Cedrick saw Mav on the ground, unconscious. He knelt beside her. He checked her pulse and quickly triaged. Cedrick looked at Willow and put his hand behind her head to make sure she was focused. "Listen to me. I think she'll be alright. We've got to get cover. Radio your daddy. Tell him to find us in Romeo Six Alpha and bring a medic. Got it?"

Willow nodded and picked the handheld radio up from the ground. It still worked. Cedrick picked Mav up off the ground and stood up. "Follow me. Stay close."

They started running through the woods. Mav was bouncing up and down in Cedrick's arms as he ran. Willow was close behind. Another volley of missiles thundered overhead.

"What's going on? Who's doing this?" Willow yelled to Cedrick.

"They're cruise missiles. They're hittin' our positions and decoys. The missiles, I ain't too worried about. We spotted a couple Warthogs flying around. They'll probably hit next."

"What's a Warthog?"

"It's an airplane, Sweetheart! It'll make for a really bad day."

***

Stan nearly fell off the ladder on his hasty descent. He ran inside the house and searched frantically for his phone. He called out to Reese to check on them. He could hear one or both boys crying.

He found his phone on the table. No service. He began to pace as he tried resetting his phone. He placed his hands on his head. "Think! Think!" he grunted aloud. He couldn't leave Reese and the boys home alone. He couldn't take them out there either. He had no idea where in the woods Maverick was. He wouldn't even know where to look. Missiles struck close to the river. Intrusive thoughts stabbed his consciousness, telling him she was dead. Lexi was at the grocery store. Missiles hit in that direction, too. "Think! Think!"

"The radio!" He yelled to himself.

***

Lexi opened her eyes and saw the sky. She was lying on her back on the pavement covered in shards of safety glass. One of the National Guard soldiers knelt down over her, checking her vitals. She looked into his eyes and could see he was shouting. She couldn't understand his muffled voice. Her ears were ringing. He reached into his belt and withdrew a small, white paper packet. He cracked it in half and put it under her nose. Her nostrils instantly felt on fire, and she came to. She could hear the thundering sound still flying overhead. People were screaming. She looked around.

Her chin was pulled forward by the soldier, his face was right in hers. "We need to move. Can you get up?"

Lexi moved her legs. She nodded. The soldier got up and ran toward the entrance of the grocery store. Several bodies were still lying on the ground. Some were squirming, and some were lifeless. The soldiers were checking each of them and trying to wake or revive those they could and help everyone find cover.

Lexi slowly rose to her feet. Glass shards were embedded deep in her forearms. Blood was dripping slowly down her arms. She couldn't feel any pain. She ran over to the soldiers and others lying on the ground. Two of the soldiers were lifting and carrying the wounded civilians inside the Food Towne building to find cover. The soldier who helped her wake up was checking each of the bodies that were not moving.

"Help move some of them inside," He yelled.

Lexi nodded. She walked up to an older woman lying on the pavement and bent down over her. Her head was bleeding.

"Not her!" He pointed at several bodies. "They're all dead. Help over there. We need to get away from the vehicles."

A woman was wandering aimlessly. Lexi ran up to her. The woman was crying hysterically and covering her ears, walking in circles. She put her arm around the woman, trying to get her to walk toward the building. The woman screamed. Above them, two aircraft flew over at low altitude. Drones were passing overhead as well. Every time something flew overhead, Lexi felt numb and dizzy.

She was able to help the woman get inside. As she walked back outside to help the remaining wounded, an aircraft in the distance was launching missiles toward the industrial part of town. Booms from the missiles striking in the distance made the glass shards on the ground vibrate and bounce. The aircraft was flying back and forth, making circles in the sky. The engine's scream was terrifying.

The soldier ran up to Lexi and grabbed her shoulder. "That's an A-10 Warthog. It's probably knocking out armored vehicles. I'm sure they've got bigger fish to fry, but we need to get away from the Humvees just in case. Come on, let's go!"

The warthog twisted and rolled in the sky. It turned toward their direction and got closer. The high-pitched scream was deafening. The nose of the aircraft began to puff white smoke like a cigarette. A second later, a loud sound growled from the cannon, making an explosion on the ground in the distance.

"We need to go, now!" The soldier shouted. Lexi quietly followed.

***

Maverick was starting to wake up. She was in Cedrick's arms as he was jogging and out of breath. Willow was close behind. Explosions, screaming sounds of aircraft, and drones continued in the distance.

"Here!" Cedrick yelled. He crouched down and slowly walked through a thick brush covering, completely unnoticeable to the casual observer. The small earth tunnel was reinforced with wood beams. It resembled a mineshaft and went down lower into the earth the deeper they walked. Even Willow, who was less than five feet tall, had to bend down to avoid hitting her head.

The shaft led to a larger opening that contained several cots, chairs, and tables. Boxes of various supplies were neatly organized.

"What is this place?" Willow asked, still panting from the run.

"It's a patrol base we use if we need it. We've got several."

"Is she okay?"

Cedrick set Mav on a cot. He checked her pulse again and took a flashlight to look into her eyes. "I don't know. We need a medic."

"What about my mom and dad?"

"They're fine. We knew this was comin'."

"How?"

Cedrick opened a first aid kit and dumped the contents onto a table. "Well, Sweetheart, most of us were in the military and we know how the military works. They're mostly hittin' decoys. What we wanted them to hit. We've got some good counter-intelligence folks on our side."

"Is it just in the woods?"

"Nope, they're hitting everything we took. Better to be blown up than in our hands. We've got to fight a different kind of war. *Operation Friendly Neighbor* is officially over, I'd say."

***

Stan was huddled in the bathroom with Reese, Leo, and Blaze. The boys were holding each other, lying in the bathtub, quietly whimpering. Reese sat at the edge of the tub. Her arms were folded. She looked worried and angry.

"Mom and Maverick?" Reese said, knowing the answer already.

"Phone's dead. Bob's usually on the radio. I don't hear anyone talking. I have this pocket radio too. I don't know what to do."

Stan turned on the pocket radio that was set to an FM station. The emergency response tone was chiming. Finally, an automated voice began to speak:

The Emergency Broadcast System is issuing an imminent warning to all 100 counties in the State of North Carolina...

"I'm scared—" Leo cried out as Reese held his face and tried to shush him.

...Seek immediate shelter, go to a basement or center of the building, close all windows and doors and stay inside until authorities provide further instructions.

They sat staring at the floor. The HAM radio came to life. Bob had given an update to anyone listening on *The Neighbors* channel after connecting with his usual sources on the HAM radio. He said the government, using the *Insurrection Act*, had taken action to suppress rebellion. This was a joint operation in five different states. The war had begun.

Stan felt hopeless. He sat thinking of how he failed at his most important objective, keeping his family together at a time when they needed to stay together the most. War had erupted, and no one was safe. His new task was to reunite his family as soon as possible, assuming they were alive. He felt like Maverick was right. He was ignorant and careless, and he paid the price. His family was now torn apart, and all that mattered to him was bringing his family back together, no matter the cost.

About The Author

Jason Drew Anderson is a clinical social worker and pediatric psychotherapist. He graduated from California State University Sacramento with a master's degree in social work in 2004. He specializes in cognitive behavioral therapy and has spent his career working with children and adults to overcome anxiety and depressive symptoms.

As an author, Jason's stories are thematically in support of everyday people's innate ability to overcome insurmountable odds through courage, suffering and growth by focusing on what we can control in our lives. The characters are true to life and must take inventory of their strengths and bolster their deficits. Jason enjoys writing about scenarios commonly feared in the modern age as an imaginable exposure activity where we can experience the anxiety and fear from a safe distance and invoke the question, "What would I do?"

www.ingramcontent.com/pod-product-compliance
Lightning Source LLC
Chambersburg PA
CBHW032117170626
46808CB00006B/1982